Gloryhole

by
Will Ridecock

Introduction

Life is an adventure to be tasted, touched, and experienced. It is my hope that you will find the short stories in this collection enjoyable and fun.

©2020 Ocotillo Press

ISBN 978-1-954285-03-3

Printed in the United States of America
Second Printing, 2020

Ocotillo Press
Houston, TX 77017
books@ocotillopress.com

Disclaimer: This is a work of fiction. Names, characters, places, and incidents either are the products of the author's imagination or are used fictitiously. Any resemblance to actual persons, living or dead, businesses, companies, events, or locales is entirely coincidental.

Feedback, Comments, and Story Requests should be sent to: books@ocotillopress.com
NOTE: All submissions become the property of the publisher, Ocotillo Press.

Chapters

Fucked by the Fire Inspector

He was here. I saw him maneuvering his government issued vehicle and backing into my driveway like he always did. I briefly thought back thinking of how many times this guy had come over and fucked my ass and buried his seed in me. I had first found him via a Craigslist ad. It was titled something along the lines of "fuck and seed my ass." I normally got flakes off this particular posting, but this guy was not a flake.

He insisted on fucking me anonymous. I was naked, cleaned out, and lubed up. I would be face down on a sleeping bag in the middle of my garage waiting on him to fuck me. What he didn't know is that I would watch through a crack in the fabric I had hung in the garage window. That helped me minimize my "down time" face down ass up on the garage floor waiting for his thick latin dick. Every time was the same game. I would watch him back in and then I would slip some more lube in my ass and get face down on the sleeping bag. I kept my end of the deal and never directly looked at him. He would walk in to the garage and strip down out of his uniform. Carefully putting his uniform on a chair that I had nearby for him. He was Latino, probably Puerto Rican or mixed Spanish/White. He was hung with a 7.75-8 inch thick cock and he liked to fuck. Hard, Deep, and long enough to bust a nut, but not so long as to make me bored. It was always dick in ass, pounding until he nutted. No talking, no kissing, and no looking at him. Always no looking at him. For a while he was in the routine of fucking me a couple of times a week. I knew roughly what time and I basically had to be ready when the request came in.

He was like a freight train in some ways, silence preceding a storm of fucking, followed by silence after he left. I quickly made my way across the garage floor. I hated having dust on my feet, so I stopped to wipe them quickly on the towel on the floor before getting on the sleeping bag. Dirt on the sleeping bag always found it's way into the lube on my cock. I love to jack off while I'm getting fucked.....

I set the lube on the cement block I used as an altar during sex. I jokingly call it an altar. It is always in front of me and has a bottle of lube and two bottles of poppers. One is a primary and the other is a backup in case the primary spills. I then quickly grabbed the primary and inhaled deeply. I felt the poppers take hold, loosening my hole. I always called this moment "descent," as I descended into sex. One breath isn't usually enough. So I hit the poppers two more times. Holding the last breath deeply to ensure maximum impact. I then assumed the position.

Seconds later the door opened and in strode my latin cock freight train. He slipped the door quietly behind him and strode over to me. Without a word he undressed and got on his knees behind me. He reached over me and grabbed the lube, helping himself to a handful that he rubbed on his manhood. He set the lube back on my altar and then swiftly maneuvered himself behind me with his cock pushing against my hole.

One thing I always appreciated is that he knew what he was doing. He was an incredible intense fuck. He slowly inserted himself in me in one motion bottoming out with his balls against my hole. I took another deep breath on my poppers while he was going in. I told myself this had to help make it easier. He paused for a moment once he was all the way in and then pulled out 3/4 o
f the way. At about 3/4 of the way out he abruptly stopped and started pounding my hole. Bang Bang bang bang bang…. drilling it with his thick cock. By this time his arms were mixed in with mine. While he wasn't into kissing on the lips he would often lick my neck and ears and nibble on my shoulders. He continued this in what I call the fag missionary position…. ass up face down, top above me. After about 10 minutes he would speed up a little bit and then blow his load deep inside me. Most of the time that was it and the show was over. He would pull out, stand up, wipe off, and get dressed. After he got dressed he would mutter "Thanks." I would normally reply, "You're welcome." At which point he would walk out the door, letting it slam behind him. He would hop in his government vehicle and pull out just as quickly as he had arrived and backed in.

This general pattern went on for about a year. I don't remember precisely what happened, but at some point he stopped coming by and I stopped getting his seed.

The Recycler

Do you have any loads in? That was the abrasive, somewhat rude question that blurted across Grindr. I thought, who the fuck are you? Before answering, I navigated Grindr's awful interface to view the inquisitor's profile. Hmm, I thought. Ginger and spice, how nice indeed. 27, 6'2" 190#, red head, and green eyes. I did not have any loads in yet, the universe was being flaky this afternoon. So I responded honestly with "No, you want to put one in?" Tic Toc Tic Toc no reply... oh well, another nosy Grindr flake I thought. After I had moved on to something else my phone buzzed again. A reply! "Get a load first, I only fuck cummy holes." Hmm, okay.... so I responded "Cock pic?" This was my standard line and it was pretty equivalent to show me the fucking goods. A minute or so later a couple of pictures appeared on my phone. Wow, I thought, what a nice thick white cock. How rare for Houston. I sent a picture of my ass back and queried him, "Do you like to fuck raw?" No sense in playing games, let's qualify him to see if he is going to fuck or play condom games. "yes" came back the response, followed by "Get a load and hit me up."

Thus started a game of cat and mouse that went on for a few weeks. The timing was always off, he was available when I wasn't or vice versa. Finally one day the timing lined up. I had cleaned out that morning in hopes of getting laid. I was not disappointed. Around 11am my redhead hit me up, again demanding I be bred before he would fuck me. This time I had a nearby trick interested, so I was able to broker a deal. I'd go get a load and then come home to host redhead. The source of the load wasn't bad. A 24yo black guy with a 7 inch average cock that curved slightly down. He was a pretty aggressive fuck and always nutted quickly. He was a bit of a freak and once in a while he had a buddy who wanted to play. No big deal, I was using him for his load to get to the redhead today. He didn't have to know this. I agreed to hook up with him and headed to his place to get a load. He lives in this $600/mo apartment in Pasadena, TX. It's the kind of place that has a nice sign, but the rest of the property is a shithole. I imagine that the leasing agent shops at TJ Maxx and Ross Dress for Less and considers those to be high end fashion. The gate to this 'community' is a real work of art. You have to punch in a four digit code to get in and it never works right for me. As I sat their punching in codes cars lined up behind me. Finally the latina woman behind me got out of her car and came over and told me how to put the code in. She looked impatient with her two kids in her beat the hell up Toyota mini van. I could tell she had been fucked at least twice from the two kids in the car. I wondered if her husband was a good fuck or not. As the gate finallly opened my mind snapped back to the present. I navigated the well worn parking lot full of has been cars that told the tale of their owners who lived paycheck to paycheck. I parked and locked my car and walked over to my trick's apartment. Unit #705. He always answered the door from behind the door and today was no exception. He was naked and erect when I walked in. It was dark in the apartment. We went to his bedroom which was just off the kitchen and living area. I lubed him and my ass up and the hit my poppers. He bent me over the bed and slid his cock in, stretching my hole a little as he entered me. He never wasted any time and started pumping me and moaning. I actually enjoyed the way he fucked, so I was stroking my own cock while he pumped me. He usually hit my g-spot and made me shoot my creamy load onto the carpet and side of his bed. Today was no exception. I shot my load and he kept fucking. A few minutes later he slammed his cock balls deep into me and creamed my hole. He always pulls out a few seconds later, and then the show is over. It's back to normal for him and he ushers me out as quickly as he can. As best I can tell he is some sort of security guard for a refinery or government building. He claims to be a musician too. His apartment is full of knicknacks and crap. In and of itself this wouldn't be odd, but I wonder how a 24 year old manages to decorate with this much crap. It's like a woman lives there, but other than the junk there is no real sign of a woman. I wonder about this as I navigate the cramped apartment and make my way to the door. I'm not annoyed this time and am anxious to get home and get my redhead.

As I get to the car I check Grindr to make sure we're still on. I have four messages from redhead. Fuck, I was only bent over for about 10 minutes. Four fucking messages? grrr. He's sitting in my driveway and wants to know how soon I can be there. Ugh, dammit. I pull out of Shithole Creek Apartments and head for home. I'm always careful in Pasadena not to speed. The cops are hot, but they would just assume give you a ticket as spit on you. Home is only 3 miles away, so it doesn't take me long to navigate the school zones and wierd ass streets that run at funny angles.

I'm horned up and craving his cock as I drive, and still slightly loopy from my poppers and good pounding. I pull into the driveway and see a shiny black car sitting in my parking spot. I park next to him and look over, not quite sure what to expect. Sometimes Grindr tricks are hot, and sometimes they are not. This guy is hot. Like Clark Kent hot, clean cut, buzzed haircut. Scruffy. I start to feel moist as we make eye contact. Oh I'm really wanting this and at the same time thinking, wow, what did I do to get this guy ?

As we both get out and make small talk I unlock the gate and invite him in. We walk past the pool and I unlock the bedroom French doors. I draw the blinds that are built into the doors. We

9

both start stripping and hanging our clothes on various pieces of furniture in the bedroom.

As he undresses in front of me I see that his cock really is thick and big. I'm guessing it's 4.5 around and 9 long. yum, this is going to be a great fuck I think. I drop down on my knees and he puts it in my mouth and starts working me over. I'm rock hard, dripping, and stroking as I suck him hard. I keep sucking him and bobbing on his cock. He's running his hands through my hair and pushing my head down on his cock to where I can hardly breath. It's intense. And then he pulls me up and asks if I still have a load in my ass. Of course I reply. He pushes me over the bed and drops down on his knees. Before I can ask what he's doing he is sniffing my ass. I think wow, he's checking. As I start to ask him about it he sticks his tongue into my crack and starts eating me out. He's clearly done this before and he's pretty good at it. My hole instinctively opens a bit as he probes it with his tongue. It feels like he is licking the cum out of my ass!

After a few minutes of this he stands up and puts the head of his cock against my ass. I turn to put some lube on him and he stops me and holds me against the bed. He says to me, "The cum from the other guy is my lube, you'll take it like this." With that he pushes inside me and I inhale deeply on my poppers as he stretches and invades my ass. I'm loving every second of it. He starts working in and out going deeper with each thrust until he is balls deep. At that point he shifts and starts pounding my ass for a few minutes. We are both turned on and having hot intense sex. As he seems to be getting close he stops and pulls out. Without a word he lays down on the bed and moves to the center of my king size bed. I follow him up on the bed and climb on top of him. He maneuvers me over his cock and sits me down on it. I begin to slowly rock up and down on his meat as he is tweaking my nipples and I'm playing with his furry red chest hair. I lean down to kiss him and he quickly turns away, signaling that he doesn't kiss. Too bad I was already falling for him imagining trying to date this big dicked kinky freak.

After several minutes of riding him and nuzzling and groping each other he pushes me over and off of him. He gets up on his knees and moves me face down and ass up in front of him. I correctly anticipate him sliding in me, but this time he's holding me down and really pounding my ass. It's good, it's deep, and it's big. Wow, it's a great piece of meat between his legs. After a few minutes of this he pushes in and I can feel his cock pulse as he creams my hole. He lays there for a minute or two with his cock inside me, surrounded by his seed which is deep inside my ass. Then he slowly pulls out and climbs out of bed.

We don't talk much. I wipe down and offer him a clean towel. He wipes up and starts getting dressed. Neither of us says anything. As he gets ready to go I thank him and suggest we should do it again. He says he enjoyed it and we'll see.

Fluffy's Torpedo

It had taken forever to get checked in. The new clerk at Mid-towne Spa was having trouble with the old computer. When I finally got to him I could tell he was flustered, so I tried to be as nice as possible. He issued me the key for room 501. I locked up my wallet and my car keys and trotted up the stairs to my assigned den of iniquity. I normally didn't go to the bathhouse on a Friday. It was usually too busy for me to effectively get dick. I was bored tonight and horny, so after hours of getting knowhere on Grindr I had cleaned out and headed off to the baths.

On my way to my room I passed the normal menagerie of characters that made Midtowne unique and fun. I saw my "friend" who liked to chat about the plight of corporate workers while waiting for a nice dick to suck. We both worked corporate jobs and he was a nice guy to chat with. I said "hi" to him and he said "hi" back. Ships passing in the night, I strode to my room, anxious to get undressed and start prowling.

I reached my assigned room. I swore every room had a different lock, this one was no different. It took me three tries before I convinced the tired ass lock to open up and let me in the room. Johnny had done a great job getting my room ready. Johnny was the hardest working Latino floor guy the World had ever known. Friendly, polite, and cleaned like a Catholic. He always worked evenings. I felt sorry for him, but really appreciated his hard work. My room had a small paper bag for a trash can, a light switch, a "mattress" and a pastel sheet. It wasn't much, but it was enough to lay down on, relax on, and get fucked on. It would do the trick, or hopefully tricks. I stepped in and shut the door behind me. I put my bag on the "table" that was built in and stripped off my shirt and sweatpants. I tossed them on the bag and placed my phone next to my backpack. I opened the side pocket and fished out my Uranus Wet Lube and my collection of poppers. After briefly looking at them I picked the one that would put me in my place and took a short hit on it. I then lubed up my ass and cock. I grabbed my towel, put my key around my arm and picked up my lube and poppers before heading out the door. It was time to prowl.

I headed back to the maze to see what was going on. This maze was dark and usually had some fucking going on. It was one of the things you could count on at Midtown. The ceiling fan desperately needed to be ripped down. It had long ago stopped working and was hanging at an angle, covered in dust. A single, bare red light bulb lit the maze area with some rope lights thrown in for ambiance. I surveyed the men. A competing Latin bottom, a Black cock sucker, and a white power bottom were in attendance. The obligatory not into you black guy with the 9 inch cock and the slim shady looking for head were wandering through every couple of minutes. I decided to setup shop by standing with my cock in my hand leaning forward against the wall. This left my ass out and kept my cock away from creepy dick grabbers. I liked to slowly massage my cock and judge how turned on something or someone made me as I thought about the possibility they represented.

After a minute or so Fluffy appeared. Fluffy was… well fluffy. A big big black guy, about my height and probably double my weight. I admired his courage in coming in here and wondered what he was into. Certainly not my type, I was keeping myself amused by watching him. He slid down the narrow walk way towards me, being unusually polite to the other guys. As he approached me I could tell he was staring at my ass. This made me mildly uncomfortable because I was being setup to have to let him down easy and encourage him to move along. I'm into getting fucked…. and fat guys usually don't have enough dick to interest me. Sorry, it's just how it is. Kitty has needs and you needs to be able to get in kitty to meet them.

I was right, he was laser focused on my ass. He slowed down when he got to me and stopped directly behind me. I could kind of see him out of the corner of my eye, but I really could feel the heat coming off of him. I realized he was probably within a foot of me and still staring intently at my ass. His big broad hand reached out and started to caress my back and shoulders. He had a nice touch, but he had to be all of at least 350. He was fat! I did not want to cause a scene, so I let him continue to rub my back. Besides, it felt good. After a few minutes he moved closer to me.

As he moved closer I felt IT. I gasped a little as his cock bumped my ass. His body wasn't touching me, but his cock was. My hole puckered a little and my hand reached down to see what this was. I gently placed my hand around the shaft of his cock and stroked it a bit to get a feel for his size. Oh My God Becky! This was a BIG cock. It was probably 10 inches and a happy handful around. I wondered in my mind if I could take it. I wasn't sure, but I was gonna fucking find out.

At about that moment I decided to move into a cubby space and bend over. I motioned for Fluffy to follow me and he willingly did. I quickly lubed my hole, his cock, my dick, and his cock again. And then I hit my poppers like some asthmatic kid on an inhaler trying to save his life. I needed to loosen my hole up, like 5 seconds ago. Godzilla was coming! It crossed my mind that I was about take a cock that was attached to someone I didn't find terribly attractive. But this was a fuck not a date and I didn't really give a shit. My hole was twitching and wanting to be stretched and plowed. I was standing in front of fluffy and he was standing behind me and "occupying" the entrance to the cubby. One good thing I thought is that nobody was going to get past him. I hated "interference" from desparate queens who would stick their hands in and try to grab the tops dick while you were getting fucked.

As I bent over Fluffy put the head of his cock against my ass and started to push. At first my ass wasn't having any of it. A vision of the Panama canal locks flashed through my mind, holding back a huge ship behind massive doors. As if on queue, Fluffy turned up the pressure and broke down the doors to my ass. Expertly he pushed just the head in which caused my hole to tighten up and grip his cock. He stopped and started rubbing my shoulders again which relaxed me. This was his queue to start to pull back and then push a little deeper. He continued this for a few minutes working his massive black meat into my stretched white hole.

The whole time I had been sniffing poppers like it was some sort of religious sacrament. In a way it was.... .the incense of the horny bottom worshipping the big meat God. I think he was probably half way in when it happened. He suddenly stopped being nice and it's like someone opened the throttle. He started pile driving my ass. Not all at once, but it went from pull and push to thump..... thump..... thump thump... thump thump thump. Next thing I knew I was being fully assaulted from behind. He was slamming his cock deep in my hole and shaking my whole body. I'm not a little guy, but I'm not fat either. I'm 5'11" 205# and built okay. I was being pushed around by the black meat in my ass like some sort of rag doll. My head was periodically hitting the wall in front of me and at some point he got all the way in because I remember his balls starting to slap my ass. He was like one of those piledriving machines you see on the construction sites just banging his pole deeper into my hole. He showed no sign of climaxing or getting anywhere near ready to bust a nut in my hole.

No good deed goes unpunished and by this time a crowd had gathered behind him to watch him wreck my ass. Sex in the maze is sometimes spontaneous and I could catch glimpses and hear the signs that several other cocks were getting worked nearby. On the one hand I hoped there was a line forming, and on the other my mind was writing checks that my ass would be too worn out to cash. I was aware of a burning sensation that was building in my ass and what I can only describe as "surf" the sensation when your guts have been churned and you aren't sure what is about to happen next. You just know that it won't be something nice. Fluffy kept right on pounding my ass like some kind of mechanical beast, periodically telling my what a nice white boy ass I had. I did my best to mutter yes sir, and fuck my hole. I would periodically ask if he was going to breed me, or if he was getting close. Over the course of 20 minutes this disintegrated into alternating pleas for his seed and warnings that kitty was going to need a break.

He got rougher as time went on and finally had me pinned between his meat and the wall pumping me like some sort of invader. Almost anti-climatically he warned me that he was about to nut in my ass and then a few strokes later I felt it. It was like he had turned on a hose and his seed gushed into my hole filling me up and dripping out. He pulled out almost immediately pulling some of his seed with him. It followed his cock out and hit the floor with a loud splash. I was a bit embarassed but it was dark and nobody could tell what it was. He said "Thanks white boy" and walked off leaving my totally wrecked, seeded hole gasping for breath against the wall of the cubby hole. Whatever sort of line might have formed scattered like pigeons before a cat when Fluffy's load unceremoniously squirted partly out of my ass and hit the floor with a loud noise. So there I was in the maze, alone, with cum running down the inside of my thighs listening to blaring dance music and trying to reconcile that a fat guy with a monster cock had just wrecked my ass. Not one to miss a moment I decided this was my queue to exit. I wiped my legs and ass with my towel and briskly walked off towards my room to rest and recover.

I never saw Fluffy again after he wrecked my pussy.

Too Tall Fucking

Sometimes after a long day it's nice to go to Midtowne Spa and unwind. Monday was one of those days. Half price rooms are a good thing and traffic was light on the way in. I parked without any trouble and went in. The staff is friendly and it's like seeing an old friend most of the time when I get to the counter. I said high to the kinky old guy who was working the desk and asked for a regular room, preferably one with hung tops. He chuckled and asked if 406 would work? I told him that was fine and paid my $10 and change.

I went up to my room, undressed, lubed my ass and opened up a new bottle of poppers. I always like to pre-lube my ass before I go prowling. It helps ensure a slippery fuck. I decided to open a new bottle from US Pop Shop... their poppers are smooth and different from the PWD stuff I order online. Sort of a little treat to offset the stupidity of a long workday.

I grabbed my poppers, lube, and towel, put my key around my arm and strode out the door to see what I could find. On the way there I noticed a really tall black guy pacing in a hall but fully dressed. It was busy for a Monday but quiet in the maze area. There was a stocky white guy who looked like he might be kinky. The problem with 20-somethings is you just never know if they want to fuck or still are working through their bullshit. I decided to just pick a spot and see if he hit on me.

After a few minutes I decided it would be better for me to pick a different spot. I like to stand with my ass out facing a wall at a corner. This lets me keep an eye out, but leaves my ass open for passing tops to grab and show they are interested. I jokingly think of it as setting the cookies out. It rarely disappoints. I had been there for under 5 minutes when too tall came by. I knew he was walking around the glory hole booths and could tell he was prowline for ass. When he did come around the back where I was at he predictably stopped and his hand landed on my ass. He deftly worked his finger in my crack and found it was prelubed. He pushed his rough finger against my hole a few times and I just relaxed. He leaned over my shoulder and growled "105" in my ear. I knew that this meant to meet him at his room, number 105.

If you go to a bathhouse enough, the rooms begin to take on a personality. 105 definitely had a personality. I had gotten dicked good in that room a few times, so I was excited. I took my time getting there and found him just opening the door when I arrived. I followed him in without a word. He shut the door behind me and I realized it was really dark, more so then usual in this room.

I hit my poppers, lubed my hole and set my towel and stuff on the end of the mattress. He was getting undressed and I knew what was next. I dropped to my knees and he put his floppy cock in my mouth. It tasted nasty, but I kept sucking it. Any temptation to take it out of my mouth and ask what was on it was gone when he grabbed my head and started face fucking me. He had not said a word to me since I got here and I could tell this was going to be a good fuck. He was probably about 8.5, average thickness, but he had it crammed down my throat. His bushy pubes were against my face and rubbing my nose. Some guys have a smell to them and this guy was definitely musty. I was beginning to choke a bit, but he didn't care, he was fucking my face working towards getting fully erect.

Just as quickly as he had started he stopped. He pulled me up and pushed me towards the bed. I hit my poppers hard and spread some lube on his cock. I did manage to get two squirts of lube on his dick before he pushed me over the bed and began working his way in. He wasn't particularly gentle the way some guys are. He was here to fuck and it was really obvious that he was using my hole for that purpose.

He had one big hand on my hips, his cock deep in my ass, and then he took his other hand and put it between my shoulders. He pushed me all the way down on to the mattress. Meanwhile he was pounding my ass and finally getting more vocal. Mainly consisting of moans and take it boy's. I was pinned down on the bed and able to just work myself around to where I could look back between my legs. This afforded me the opportunity to periodically hit my poppers when he would pause. Otherwise I was watching his legs come towards me and away from me as he proceeded to wreck my hole.

This went on for a good 20 minutes and he was tearing my ass up. If felt like he was churning my insides with a stick! I was still basically pinned on the bed. He would periodically stop and his giant hands would swoop down and push my knees together, forcing my ass higher. I finally figured out that this was more convenient for him because he was tall. I had wedged my head against the wall to keep from being banged into the wall. As he would push I would feel him push against me, pushing me into the wall and I could hear the other wall being pushed behind him. For a second I wondered what others might think… and then I decided to egg him on a little bit. Sometimes talking shit gets you a load of cum faster.

I told him he was tearing me up. No response. I told him to use that ass. No response, no change. I told him I needed a break soon. No you don't, came the reply. I quietly said, yes I do. He leaned over me and said, "No, You don't! I'm not done with you, take it." and with that he was holding me down and seemingly doubled up on pounding my ass. He was shoving it in and then working his cock around like he was going to find some sort of god damn prize. For the tops reading this I promise you don't want the prize that this produces. I muttered that I needed to stop soon. He ignored me and just kept fucking. Bang, bang bang sweep, bang bang sweep.

Finally he thrust in, moaned, and I felt his cock pulse a few times as he bred my hole and filled it with his seed. He pulled out and stood against the wall for a second. I grabbed my towel, poppers, and lube. At about that moment the door opened which I knew was my queue to get the fuck out. I wasted no time in leaving. As I walked away the door to 107 opened revealing a very hot black guy. He looked at me and looked me up and down. I guess he had been watching me get fucked. It's possible to stand on the mattress and see over the wall into the next room. I paused to see if he was going to invite me in, and he retreated into his room, shutting the door.

My hole was drippy and I knew that it was time to go sit in the hot tub for a few minutes.

Flipper

I had spent about an hour sitting in the hot tub and relaxing in the pool. I was chatting with this other Amateur Radio Operator. It was nice to engage in casual intelligent conversation from time to time. I looked up at the clock and realized it was 10 something. I dried off and headed up to my room for a drink.

I was torn over leaving or getting another load. My pussy had been thoroughly wrecked a little earlier that evening. Always the cum-whore I decided to make a lap and see if I could get another load before I left.

I headed to the maze noting it had quieted down. I picked one of my usual spots and stood with my ass facing out, leaning against a corner gently. This allowed me to see all around me and gave tops a chance to see my ass and approach me.

I wasn't there more than 5 minutes when this early 30's black guy walked up. He made a couple of passes by me and I wondered if he was one of these damn racist guys. Nope, he was just shy. He came back and stood right behind me. He grabbed my ass and I reached back and grabbed his half-erect cock. I asked if he wanted to fuck some ass and he replied, "yes." "My room or here?", I asked. Before he could answer I replied, I'm in room 406. See you there. "ok" he said. I wasn't sure if he was really going to come.

I walked to my room and let myself in. I put my towel off to the side and set down my lube and poppers. While I was wondering if he was going to show up a shadow appeared in the door. I had left the door cracked a couple of inches. He opened the door and looked into my dark room. I greeted him and said "Hi there." He stepped in and shut the door behind himself. I dropped down and started sucking him. I then stood up and before I could turn around he grabbed me and pulled me into him. We started kissing and making out which is always a bonus. We did this for a few minutes and I could feel his cock pushing against me. I couldn't stand it and lubed him up and bent over in front of him. His cock curves gently upwards, but he was pretty experienced. He slid it in and started pumping my ass good. After a few minutes I asked if he liked to be ridden. He said yes and I asked if I could. He said sure and pulled out.

I moved out of the way and let him lay down before getting on top of him. We started making out and I was grinding against his cock. Then I lifted myself up and he maneuvered his cock against my hole. I eased down on to his ass noting that it burned a little. This meant my ass was torn up real good by the previous guy, too tall. Fortunately this guy was somewhat more conventional. I bounced up and down on his shaft and he pumped my hole from below. This went on for a few minutes. It was beginning to tire me out…. so time to change positions. I stopped and made out with him for a few minutes. He grabbed my dick and stroked it a bit. As a bottom I usually don't get turned on. But something about this guy had me going. He asked if I liked to top, to which I said sure, sometimes. There was a twinkle in his eye, so I asked if he wanted to get fucked right now. He said yes, so I maneuvered myself between his legs. I grabbed some lube and lubed his hole. Next I offered him some poppers before I hit them myself. Then I slipped the head of my cock inside him while leaning forward to make out with him some more.

He moaned softly as I slipped in him. I wasted no time getting all the way in him. He had a nice tight hole and he was very sensual. It was refreshingly good sex for the baths. I started slowly but before long was pounding his hole. After a few minutes of pounding his ass I slammed my cock in and unloaded in him. Then I collapsed on top of him nuzzled against his neck. He was caressing my shoulders and it really felt great.

After a few minutes I realized that he had precum quite a bit and I could feel his cock periodicallly throbbing against my stomach. I knew that I still owed him my hole.

I suggested that we try me face down ass up for him to breed and he agreed. I maneuvered into position and he slipped behind me and inside me. He began to pump me and then stopped after a couple of minutes. I asked if he was edging and he said yes. I told him I wanted his load next time. He held his cock in side me still. After a minute or so he started pumping again. This went on for a couple of minutes before he started to edge again. I squeezed down on his cock with my muscular ass and begin to push back against him working his shaft. This pushed him over the edge and he resumed pounding me until he shot his load. I felt a good 3 squirts come out of him and deep up in my ass. We both lay there quietly. Me on my stomach and him on my back inside me. His cock felt fantastic, even if I was a little bit sore.

As with all good things he slid out and stood up. I rolled over and turned the light on a bit. I asked what area he lived in and was pleasantly surprised it was my side of town. He wasn't as handsome in the light, but he was very good in bed and I didn't give a damn. I grabbed my phone and opened the contacts. I asked if he wanted to get together sometime. He said sure and I asked for his phone number. I sent him a text and told him I looked forward to it.

20

I noticed his cock was still sticking straight out with a gentle curve up. I needed to get home and eat, so I whisked him out the door despite the temptation to ride him for another load. Hopefully I will hear from him soon.

Ass Pounder

I slipped the key into room 503 and jiggled the lock. The well worn lock resisted at first. As the pin tumblers engaged the lock begrudgingly let me in. I was horny as hell and it had been slow getting laid lately. The night before had been a complete waste of time. I tossed my backpack in the corner and quickly stripped down. I tossed my clothes on top of the backpack and pulled out my lube and poppers. I lubed my ass hoping it was mostly clean. I had cleaned out prior to leaving the house and thought I was good to go. As luck would have it I barely made it to my counselors office. The rough road had jiggled my insides. I barely got to the toilet before my gut let go. That usually meant things wouldn't be squeaky clean.

I grabbed my towel and headed for the bathroom to piss. I figured I would go down to the hot tub and at least soak for a few minutes and let the hot chlorine water wash my ass good.

As I entered the bathroom a black man was walking out. He was built like a Mack truck and smiled at me. I smiled back and darted to the urinal.

After finishing my business I decided to walk around and see who was here. I couldn't quite tell if my gut was done tormenting me or not. I absolutely hated being a messy bottom, but didn't see much of a choice.

I was beginning to think maybe it was dead. I walked through the maze and didn't see anyone. I rounded the corner and headed back towards my room. About 1/3rd of the way down the hall I saw Mr. Smiley Mack Truck. I smiled again and he smiled back. I walked a few steps past him and stopped. He had done the same thing and then started to walk back to me. He stopped next to me and asked how come I had such a nice ass. I smiled and said, "Thanks, want to fuck it and find out how nice it feels?" I grabbed his cock and felt how thick it was. He said, "Sure." I replied, "room 503." I turned and walked to my room with him in close pursuit.

We both walked into my room and he threw his towel on the bed by the door. I tossed mine on my bag and turned to him. I dropped to my knees and started sucking his cock. It was even bigger than I had expected, probably 5 wide and a touch over 9 long. He adjusted his cock ring and started to gently work my mouth and throat. After a few minutes he pulled me up and told me to bend over the bed.

I grabbed my lube and poppers hastily. I lubed my ass up

22

and lubed his cock good. It was damn big and I wasn't sure if I could handle this as my first dick for the night. I took a couple of deep breaths from my poppers and then got on all fours facing the wall with my ass towards him. He placed his big thick hands on either side of my hips and pulled me gently against his cock. As I hit my poppers again and prayed this wouldn't hurt too much he pulled my hole over his cock. I felt my ass stretch and my guts churn. He was experienced and knew how to work that cock. He quickly opened my hole and wasted no time in starting to pound me. He was one of these guys who liked to bang your ass and drive his cock all the way in.

I'm not sure if my ass went numb or the poppers just kicked in, but after a minute or two of wondering if my ass was going to explode on him things evened out. He was pounding my ass good and hard. I was sure anyone else in the club knew I was getting fucked and fucked hard. He wasn't talking much and neither was I. I was moaning as he pounded me and he was moaning occassionally in response to my hole squeezing him. After about 10 minutes he stopped and just froze. I could tell he was edging now. He waited maybe a minute and then started again, slowly at first, but then quickly reaching a tempo of pounding on my hole.

This went on for a few cycles. Finally I was ready for him to cum so when he stopped to edge I started working his cock with my ass, pushing back on him. I was hoping it would push him over the edge. I was right. He groaned in pleasure and then leaned into me and started pounding me as hard as he could. After about a minute he thrust himself into me and I felt his manhood pulse as he planted his seed deep in my gut and held it there. I stayed frozen, just taking his load in. This was that good fuck I had been craving. He held his cock in me for what seemed like a long time. After probably only a minute he pulled out.

As he pulled out of my ass I felt something squirt out and thought, oh shit! I was terrified that I had just shot a blob out on his feet or the floor. I immediately apologized and turned the light on dimly. He asked what was wrong and I explained that I thought he had disturbed the order of the universe and I wasn't sure what had popped out besides his dick. He laughed and said it was probably his seed. I think he was right because I didn't see anything nasty or smell anything vile.

He told me I had a fantastic ass and that he had really en-joyed it. I told him thank you and asked if he lived nearby. He said he did and that he wanted to hit my hole again. I smiled and asked for his number. I put him in my contacts and sent him a text.

As I wrapped up I stood up and rubbed his shoulders a bit. He was covered in sweat, but built so well! I leaned in closer to him and licked his nipple. I kept licking and then nibbled a bit. I switched to the other one, enjoying playing with my ebony stud. I looked up and realized he was enjoying this as much as I was. I stood up and nuzzled his neck a bit, not entirely sure if he would return the act. Some guys were affectionate and some aren't. He didn't object at all. I worked my way up and gave him a quick kiss on the lips. This was the moment where I'd find out how affectionate he was. He didn't flinch at all. The next thing I knew we were making out hard core. He was a great kisser. Intense sex and Intense kissing were huge turn ons. Apparently not just for me either. I noticed his huge cock was hard again and so I grabbed it with my right hand and stroked it a little bit. I asked if he wanted to fuck again.

He spun me around and bent me over. Before I could reach for more lube he had pushed his cock into me. He wasted no time in opening me up. He started pounding me again and he was slamming my ass. Bang bang bang bang he kept pounding that ass and pumping me good. After about 8 minutes he stopped, leaving the tip of his cock inside me, and said he didn't think he could cum again. I asked, "Are you enjoying it?" Without replying he started pounding me again.

After about 5 minutes he stopped again and told me he wasn't going to be able to cum. I didn't ask this time, I growled back at him, "Fuck me sir!" He obliged me and started drilling my ass. I muttered to him to keep going and to use my ass.

He did. He kept drilling that ass hard, slapping his body against my ass and trying in vain to split my ass in half. After what seemed like ten minutes he managed to cum again. It was the same as before, but without the pause. It was really hot, I felt his cock get a little bigger and then noticed he got alot more intense. Then he thrust in and stopped. As he stopped his thick meaty cock started to pulse, pumping his seed deep inside me again.

He didn't hold it in for a while this time. While he was still in me he grabbed his towel and started drying off. When he got down to his midsection he pulled his cock out, wiped it off and cleaned up. He thanked me again, wrapped his towel around his body and walked out the door.

I had rolled over by now and realized the cooler air from the hallway felt fantastic flowing over the sweat on my body. After a second I snapped out of my daze and realized the door was open. I pushed it shut with my foot and laid back on the bed, just collaps-

24

ing in post-seeding exhaustion. My hole had behaved and I had just gotten that thorough fucking that every bottom longs for when they are horny.

As I lay there in the darkness, listening to dance music blaring through the speakers I heard my phone buzz. I reached for my phone and unlocked it. I had a text message already from the stud who's seed was oozing out of my ass. That was a good sign and suggested I would get bred again by him someday.

Bed Breaker

All I could hear was the droning of the cheap mini-split Air Conditioner in my bedroom. It was pitch black and I was laying face down on the bed. I had lubed my ass and hit my poppers good and hard.

My hole was twitching a little. I knew this guy was big and good. He was very muscular and didn't talk much. He was the poster child for big black dick on a hot man. I had played with him once before but wasn't able to take him all the way. He was probably a bit over 10 inches and 4.5 wide. Huge by my white boy standards.

Fortunately I had gotten better about hosing my ass out. I had found a Klean Stream attachment on Amazon and was able to thoroughly clean my ass out. I also had a secret weapon this time. I had a couple of hydrocodone 5/325's left over from a dental procedure.

He had hit me up via email earlier in the evening and offered to come over about 10. I said sure and began the process of getting ready. At about 9:30 I took both of my leftover pills, hoping they would numb my ass up good before he fucked me.

I heard a noise outside and realized he was bringing his bike up onto my deck. The deal we had was that I would be naked, lubed, and face down ass up. He would let himself in and use my hole. As the door opened I hit my poppers deep and hard.

Without saying a word he climbed on top of me and lubed his dick. He put his cock against my ass and tried to put it in. Nothing. My ass wasn't opening up. He told me to open up. My ass wasn't cooperating.

I suggested letting me sit on it. That had worked last time and was easier with a big dick. He said "ok." We swtiched positions in the dark. I lubed his cock and snorted my poppers before positioning myself over his towering cock. I slowly worked my ass onto the head of his cock. It felt like a totem pole going into me. I was sure this was going to rip me. It hurt like hell at first, but then slowly my hole relaxed. I eased down onto his cock wondering how it would feel when it was all the way inside me. It filled me up completely. Oddly it was turning me on to have this giant black manhood inside my ass. I was fully erect as I sat on him. Normally getting fucked made me go limp. But something about this muscular stud with his 10inch dick being inside me was turning me on.

As I managed to get all the way down on his shaft he reached up and grabbed me with his huge hands. He was probably 6'4" and 250# to my 5'10" and 185#. He pulled me down to him and kissed me. Oh wow this was hot. And then he started to slowly pump me from underneath. Easing in and out of my tight hole and making out with me while he did it. After a few minutes he told me to lay down face down ass up again.

He maneuvered behind me again. I glanced over at the clock which read 1:00am. This time he placed his arms around me and put his cock against my ass. He didn't hesitate, but instead pushed his cock inside me. God damn this hurt! I squirmed and struggled a bit. I told him this wasn't going to work. My pleas fell on deaf ears. He held his shaft deep in my hole and held me firm against him. After a few rounds he quietly whispered in my ear to relax and let it happen. He told me that he was in my hole and that it was going to be his. I had a choice in the matter. It was my choice if I got fucked or raped. I could keep struggling and he would rape my ass or I could stop struggling and get fucked. I paused, completely stunned for a moment. He was right, I didn't have a choice in what he did. He was totally in control. I decided to try getting fucked, even though it felt like I was being raped. I opened my bottle of poppers and sniffed them like it was oxygen inside that bottle. I swore I was trying to breath through that 1/2 inch opening in the top of the bottle.

It helped a little. After a few deep breaths I began to feel slighly dizzy and my vision narrowed a little bit. I heard his deep gravely voice again in my ear, "Good boy, do what I tell you and service my cock right." I replied, "Yes sir." He started pumping my ass, slowly at first. I kept hitting my poppers and strangely enjoying being thoroughly violated by this masculine sexy hot fucking man. He kept fucking. I glanced at the clock again, it said 1:25 now. He had been fucking me for 25 minutes.

He was getting rougher with me and the whole bed was shaking as he slammed his cock in and out of me. This was the hardest, roughest fuck I had ever had. I loved it. Then it happened. With a tremendous crash the bed protested. The footboard fell off the end of the bed and the whole mattress fell about 6 inches. He didn't let me up, but he did stop. We both laughed a little realizing that the bed had just broken. He said, "What now?" I said, "Well, it's broken and your cock has not been serviced sir, keep fucking!"

He began pounding me again. I glanced over and realized it was 1:45 now. After a couple of minutes I felt a change in his pace. He seemed more tense and I wondered what was happening. He got much rougher and harder and then slammed his cock into me and stopped. He had been quiet up to this point, but suddenly let out a loud moan as his cock pulsed and filled me with seed.

We both laid there for what seemed like forever. Finally he slipped back and stood up. I offered him a towel and grabbed another towel to wipe myself off. Without a word he wiped down and got dressed. I started to put the bed back together, he helped me out, lifting one side so we could slide the bed frame onto the footer board. We both smiled and laughed.

Without another word he turned around and walked out the door, shutting it behind him.

Tool Room

It was dicey to hit on another soldier. My gaydar told me that I could get into Smith's pants. Smith was another soldier I worked with in Ft. Wainwright, Alaska. We were both assigned to HQ CO 5/11th Artillery, 6thID. It was fucking cold out and there wasn't a damn thing to do at night, aside from throwing dollars at the dancers at the Flying Flea Carpet, our bases strip joint. I wasn't really interested in the fleas or the carpet, so I steered clear of the horny drunk soldiers being fleeced of their money.

I was supposed to be in one of the artillery batteries, I was a 13B cannon crewmember, aka Gun Bunny. Smith was a mechanic. I had just propositioned him after several days of making small talk to figure out how horny he was. I normally would ask a series of questions about the prospect's sexual experience, preference, and try to determine a Hornyness Score. The more horned up the guy was the more likely I'd get to suck him off. It usually culminated in either an indirect or direct proposition, depending on how stupid I thought he was. The stupid ones got the indirect bet based propositions. Smith was pretty smart and we'd already established that he didn't give a damn what sucked his cock as long as he got off. I had told him I could get his dick sucked by someone who was really really good. I asked him if he was interested.

It seemed like he thought about it forever. Finally, he looked around before saying, "Sure." We were both nervous, horny, and excited. He was scheduled to ETS in a couple of weeks, so this was a pretty safe proposition for me. I had nearly been court martialed for hitting on another guy a few months ago. Like a moth to a flame this faggot just wanted to suck some dick. That was about all I was into in 1992.

He asked, "Where? When?" I said, "How about now, and I know a quiet, dark, secure place." I continued, "Are you game now?" He looked around again and looked down at his now growing bulge before answering, "Yea, but not here. Not in the barracks man." I agreed, "Oh hell no, not in the barracks, come on." He smiled and I grabbed my keys.

It was medically called Plantar Fascitis, but it was my pass to wearing tennis shoes and it was why I had the keys to the tool room. My command had been somewhat puzzled about what to do with me. The stupid PA assigned to our unit operated on the principle of see no ill, tolerate no ill. This basically meant if he couldn't see it broke he didn't believe it could hurt. Plantar Fascitis basically meant I had high arches and this entitled me to an alternate assignment and tennis shoes. The tennis shoes piece infuriated my CO who transferred me to HQ Battery to get rid of me. HQ Battery didn't know what to do with me so they stuck me in the motorpool where they were short handed.

At first this went okay, but then I caught on that some funny shit was going on with parts ordering. When I asked about it, they stuck me in the tool room and made me the PLL clerk, responsible for our parts stock. I promptly organized it and made sure we have every nut and bolt our mechanics needed. I painted the floor and cleaned up all the tools. I was really good at running the tool room. By design, the tool room was secure, lockable, and private at night. Being in charge of it gave me keys to the motorpool and keys to the toolroom.

Smith and I walked over to the Motorpool. It was 10pm on a Saturday night. The place would be quieter than a graveyard. I didn't really have an excuse for being here, other than maybe needing a wrench or something. My heart was pounding as I opened the outside door. There weren't any cars in the parking lot, but I never knew who or what I would find in here. The Master Sergeant, Stevens, that ran the motorpool was a cranky old bastard from Texas. I think he knew I was a cock sucker and he was the last person I wanted to run into. We slipped inside the doorway and closed the door behind us. All good so far, only the yellow "always on" lights were on. It was dimly lit, warm, and very quiet. Just the soft hiss of air escaping from some leak somewhere in the building. Our facilities folks didn't give a shit about air leaks. Periodically the big compressor would roar to life and replenish whatever leaked out 24/7.

I looked over at Smith and we both smiled and I motioned to follow me. I told myself the lie of why we were here as we strode across the motorpool bay. I was glad I didn't see anyone as it would have fucked up my chances of getting laid tonight. When we reached the door I pulled my keys out again and opened it. We both walked in and I quietly shut the door behind us.

As the door shut, the tool room returned to pitch black. It was just us, two privates, standing in the dark in the tool room. If we got caught now we would totally be busted. My mind raced trying to figure out the next step. Apparently so did his, and he took the easy path. I heard his belt buckle clink as he undid it. I quickly undid mine and dropped to my knees. I reached over and found his cock and started to gently stroke it. No resistance. I had one hand on his cock and one hand on mine. I was rock hard and dripping. Neither of us said a word. He was hard, but not precumming.

I stroked him a few times and then gently put my lips around the head of his cock. My mouth was wet, anticipating feeling his manhood inside me. All I was thinking about right now was servicing him completely. I pursed my lips and pressed against the head of his cock. He was slightly below average, nothing to tell a story about honestly. 5 inches long, skinny, below average as cocks go. I had no idea at the time and was super excited by the chance to bob his knob. I had sucking cock down to a routine by now. I would push in a little bit, pause, pull back to the tip, push in a little further, and repeat. It was working like a charm on Smith. I finally worked my way to the base of his cock and just paused there. His shaft was all the way in my mouth, rubbing the back of my throat. I was trying to keep it off my teeth. His pubic hair was in my face, surrounding my nose. As I inhaled I took in the musk of his manhood. Hmm, delicious I thought.

Before I could pull back a little and continue sucking him he pulled back a little and then thrust in. He was fucking my face. Oh, I loved this. He was gentle at first and then picked up pace after a few pumps. I was stroking at the same time he was pumping. He moaned softly and then said, "I'm about to cum!" I doubled down on his dick and before he could pull out his cock pulsed and shot a creamy load of seed into my mouth. It tasted pretty good. Slightly sweet and that distinctive cum taste. At the same time I shot my load on the floor, between his boots.

He pulled his cock out of my mouth and remarked, "Damn that was good." Before either of us could move I heard the distinctive sound of keys being put in the lock.

I was nearly panicked. Keys being put in the door could only mean one thing. Someone was coming in! Smith's cock was hanging out of his pants and my pants were down and I was on my knees with a load of my cum in front of me.

My worst fear was about to come true. I was going to get caught sucking dick! Ugh! My heart sank as the door opened and Master Sergeant Stevens opened the door. He got the door about 3/4 of the way open before his eyes realized that there were two soldiers in the tool room, in the dark. He stopped. Smith and I froze, deer caught in the headlights of the Master Sergeant. He looked at Smith and looked at me and looked at Smith again.

Smith quickly zipped up his pants and put his cock away. I couldn't blame him. Stevens didn't say anything. I knew this was "off" so I just stayed put another second or so. If I was busted, well I was busted. Before I could try to explain he said, "Well, what have we hear, a Private Cocksucker?" My heart sank. I was damned! I kept my mouth shut to see where this would go. Smith had a look of terror on his face in the dim yellow light that was coming through the toolroom door. Stevens prodded again, "Well?" I sighed and said, "Yes Master Sergeant." Might as well go out with some glory I thought. I could see Smith react a little in shock.

Stevens looked at Smith and looked at me and then looked at Smith again and said, "Boy don't you have somewhere to be?" Smith shockingly looked at me and Stevens before replying, "Yes Master Sergeant." Stevens shot back, "Well then get there." Smith left the tool room faster than a cat escaping from a dryer. Ten seconds later it was just me with my limp cock and Stevens. I couldn't see him terribly well because he was backlit. No worries, any fear evaporated when he said, "Good, I have something for you to suck boy." He stepped in and over to me as the door shut behind him. Stevens was in good shape, white, close cut dark hair, probably 45. I wasn't into older guys in the least, but he was kinda hot. I guess that was a good thing because as the door shut I heard his belt buckle come undone. I couldn't believe this.

Before I could pinch myself his 8.5" cock hit me in the face. It was hot, thick, and big. I didn't need to be told what to do, I licked it and started to suck him. He wasn't content with this and said in a low growl, "Boy you are going to suck this cock." With that he put his two medium large hands on my head and pulled me down onto his cock. I was nearly choking, gagging on his substantial manhood. He clearly didn't give a shit. I never had pegged him as being queer. His cock slid in and out of my mouth rapidly. Choking me and fucking my throat all at once. I was nearly gagging on the deeper parts of it as he fucked me. I could smell his sweaty man-balls. I realized I was getting turned on by this. After a few minutes he stopped and told me he needed more. He told me to stand up. I did as I was told. I was facing the Master Sergeant who ran the motor pool. He grabbed my hand and put it on his cock. I obediently started stroking him. He took my hand off his cock and with the other hand he turned me around. I wondered what the hell he was doing. No worries, he made sure I knew in short order. He pushed me forward and I took a couple of steps before I cam to the parts cabinet. He was directly behind me.

He cleared his throat and spit in his hand. Without asking me he spread his spit in the crack of my ass. Again he spit in his hand and spread it in my ass. My mind was racing, I really wasn't into Anal, but I also literally wasn't in a position to argue with this man. Before I could say anything I felt the head of his cock against my ass. He told me to relax and let him in or he would pin me down and take it. I pondered the choice before replying that I wasn't used to getting fucked. He replied, "I don't give a shit, I need some private ass!" With that he thrust a bit and forced the head of his cock into my hole. It hurt, but felt good at the same time. He pulled back a bit before thrusting in a bit deeper. He was going to fuck me! It burned my ass at first, and then I realized my cock had come to life. I started to stroke it, gently at first, and then furiously. Stroking my cock distracted me from the fact that my ass was being shredded by a big white dick. Stevens clearly knew what he was doing. He had one hand on my shoulder controlling my position, and the other hand was resting on the other shoulder. I let out a moan and that hand quickly covered my mouth and he growled in my ear, "Keep quiet and take this dick!" I whimpered, "Yes sir" back.

He picked up the pace and was plowing my hole. This went on for what seemed like forever before he started pounding me so hard it was moving my whole body. I was getting ready to shoot my load and didn't know if I could hold back. No matter, he slammed into me and stopped. Before I could wonder what was going on he growled in my ear, "This ass is mine, I am claiming it with my seed." I felt his cock pump deep in my ass and I realized he was cumming in my ass. I simultaneously shot a huge load all over the side of the tool cabinet.

He slipped out and stepped back. I stayed where I was and didn't move. I couldn't believe what had just happened. I got caught sucking dick and was fucked alright, but not in the punishment sort of way I would have expected. I heard him pull up his pants and fasten his belt. He stepped over to the dimly outlined door and opened it. He turned on the light and turned to me and said, "Son, this place is a mess, grab some paper towels and clean up." "Yes Sir," I responded. Before I could say anything else he replied, "When you're done go hit the rack and get a good night's sleep." "Yes Sir," I replied again. With that he stepped out and the door slammed behind him. I quickly pulled my pants up and felt a moistness in my ass. I put my finger back there to see what the hell it was. When I pulled my finger back it was gooey and clear, I sniffed it. Cum! Wow, I had just gotten used and bred by an older man. I quickly fastened my belt and wiped my finger on my pants. I grabbed some paper towels and cleaned up the floor and cabinet. I tossed them in the trash can and grabbed the bag out of it. No need to leave evidence I figured. I locked up and put the bag in the trash and hurried back to my room. It was 11:30 now.

Stevens never said anything, and it didn't happen again. I saw Smith the next day and he asked if we were in trouble. I told him "no." He looked at me funny and I replied, "I took care of it." I smiled. He laughed and said "okay, thanks."

Animal

"NOW?" read the email. I was accustomed to getting some short emails from my craigslist postings, but this was going for broke. I replied, "cock pic? like raw?" This was my normal response to the first email anyway. It was surprising how many guys didn't read my ad or thought that the picture of their splendid cock would make me think twice. I liked raw and raw only, and it needed to be big enough to get the job done and small enough to be a possibility.

Several emails later I found myself in my garage, the lights out, a couple of sleeping bags on the floor and windows covered with some flimsy black cloth from WalMart. Two layers seemed to block out the street light and make it suitably dark. I was waiting rather impatiently for my trick to arrive. He was 5'10" 205#, black, 27, with what he claimed was 9 inches. Time will tell I thought. I normally didn't hook up with black guys, but I was horny. I didn't know it, but this encounter was going to change my opinion.

I had the driveway gate open and was peering out through a crack in the fabric. Every few minutes a car would go by and I would anxiously check to see if it was pulling into my driveway. After several drivebys, one finally did pull in. It was a ancient, beat the hell up dark green Ford Astrovan. As he applied the brakes they screeched loud enough to wake the dead. This piece of shit van looked like it had just rolled off the set of Junkyard Wars. He parked and the door groaned and creaked when he got out. I thought for a second it was going to fall off! Then he slammed it. Fuck! Geez this guy was going to let the whole neighborhood know he was here. Then just as quickly he jumped back in and started his van and backed out. Ugh, the guy who had gotten out seemed to be the right build. He backed almost to the street and then stopped and shut it down. This time he got out and walked around the front. He stopped when he came to my gate post. There he proceeded to open his pants and piss on my gate. Fucking animal!

He took a long leisurely piss and then shook it once before tucking it back in his pants. He had raggedy hair and was wearing some jeans and a well worn t-shirt. This guy could have passed for homeless. He looked about the right age, but something about him was turning me on. He had a vibe like he had been uncaged.

The next part was always iffy. He started to walk to the front of the house. This could be a disaster and was one of the reasons I watched. I quickly jumped to the door and cracked it open. I loudly whispered, "Hey! Hey! Over here….." He stopped in his tracks, looked around, and then realized where the voice was coming from.

He turned and strode over to the door. He paused a second when he reached the door. I could see this in the dim light coming through the crack under the door. The door didn't have a threshold and had about a 1.5" gap. It had never been an issue in the past. Everyone always paused to get up their nerve the first time they came to play in my garage.

I was about 10 feet from the door, on my knees, nude, and with my hole lubed up. He pulled the door open and stepped in, letting it close quietly behind him. "Hello," I said. "Are you the hole I'm here for?" came the reply. "Yes sir," I shot back.

He took what seemed like two steps and unbuttoned his pants. HIs cock was all of 9 inches and maybe a little more. He had a strong masculine musty smell. His cock was flopping in my face. I wasted no time in gently taking it in my mouth and stroking it with one hand. While I was sucking him hard his pants fell to the floor and he kicked his shoes and the pants off. He took his shirt off and I could barely see that he was built and well defined. It didn't take long for me to suck him hard. I instinctively reached for the lube and slathered my hole with it before coating his big cock.

I turned around and positioned myself on all fours. Inhaling my poppers hard I was expecting to have my hole wrecked. I wasn't to be disappointed, but first a detour. My stud dropped down behind me and instead of forcing himself in me he surprised me. I felt his hot wet tongue in my ass and was surprised. It felt really good. I could smell him behind me but had not expected to be eaten out. He didn't seem to care that there was a bunch of lube down there. It was getting me turned on, I was craving his dick.

After a few minutes he had me moaning and wanting more. He asked for the lube and I passed it back. I heard him lube up and then the bottle closed. He put the head of his cock against my ass and reached up with both hands to pull me back onto him. In one slow, steady motion he inserted himself inside me. I gasped a bit, even though I was turned on and had hit my poppers he was still big and thick. Once he bottomed out he stopped and held me on him. My hole contracted a couple of times and I felt him pulse once. He said in a deep quiet voice, "I'm going to enjoy your pussy and you are going to enjoy my cock." I couldn't quite place his accent, but I definitely was enjoying his cock.

He started slowly pumping me, full deep thrusts followed by pulling nearly all the way out. It was enough to make me cum actually. Normally the show is over if I cum. But he kept on fucking. It was an opportunity for me to lay flat on my stomach. He positioned himself over me at this point and begin to pick up tempo. In no time flat he had escalated to pounding my ass. I think at one point he was trying to split me in half. Pile driving my hole with his cock. He was sweating heavily and making me moan. We were inches from the garage door which was uninsulated and only 15 or 20 feet from the fence with the neighbors. I was a bit worried they could hear us fucking if they were in their yard. On the other hand, I didn't give a shit. I had a thick black cock in my ass and the animal it belonged to was mating my hole.

This went on for 20 minutes at which point I was beginning to get sore. I asked if he was close. He said not yet and kept pounding my hole. I asked again, to which he said not yet. He was a rough fuck and my hole was worn out at this point. I told him I was going to need a break. He replied, "You'll get one when I leave." He increased his tempo and his arms reached around me. I wasn't sure if he was pinning me down or hugging me tightly. Either way he slammed his cock deep in me and injected his seed inside me. As he was cumming he said, "I own this hole now, it's mine." I said, "Yes sir."

He rolled off of me after he came and lay there for a minute. We lay side by side in the dark garage, letting the cool air circulate around us and cool us off. He pulled me over and on top of him. I lay there with my head on his chest. He was rubbing my shoulders and making me moan again. I felt his manhood pushing against me which was how I realized that my moaning turned him on. It didn't take much of this before he was fully hard and I was fully wanting it. I lifted myself up and looked him in the eyes and asked, "Do you want it again sir?" He pulled me in and kissed me and said, "yes I do." I lifted myself up and maneuvered to put his cock against my ass. He pushed up and inside me at the same time I eased down on him.

As he reached full depth I leaned back and squeezed down on him. He was banging me from underneath and came after about five minutes. I climbed off of him and lay next to him. I realized he was one of these guys who takes a while to cum the first time and then cums quickly each additional time. The rarest of the four cummers. We laid there for about fifteen minutes. We chatted a bit and he told me he was an office manager. I really liked the sex and realized I probably wouldn't see him again.

He climbed on top of me again and I felt his cock against my ass. It wasn't against it for long. He slid in and started pounding me again. Like the last time he only took about 5 to 7 minutes to climax. This was his 3rd load in me tonight. My hole was sore and wrecked, but dripping his seed.

When he was done he asked for a towel and wiped himself down and got dressed. He said "Thanks." I replied, "Sure thing." and he walked out the door letting it slam behind him. He climbed into his piece of trash Astrovan and backed out. That was the last I ever saw of him.

Morning Stray

Bzzzz. Bzzzz. My phone was making a slight buzzing noise. I cracked my eyes open and rolled over to find the offending object. I grabbed it and unlocked it. It was a Grindr Message. The sender was a 27yo handsome black guy. Hmm, that's a nice way to wake up I thought. I said Hi back and layed there. It was 8:45am according to the digital clock on my dresser. Ugh, I needed to get going.

I checked my phone again, first meeting wasn't until 10am so I was good to go for a few minutes. My day was packed with conference calls, the new normal. Fortunately I could work from home most of the time, so this left me time for breakfast.

"I want some ass, now!" read the message. "cock pic?" I replied. A very nice thick, black cock came back in the image that responded. "Host or visit?" I replied. "You host, location?" he replied. I sent back my location and a couple of pictures of my ass. "address?" he replied. I thought for a second about my roommate who was asleep upstairs and then sent my address. I asked my trick if he wanted to fuck out in my motorhome or in my house. He replied that he didn't care, I just needed to lubed and ass up. I told him he would be fucking me in my motorhome. I asked his ETA and he responded 16 minutes.

I hurried through the shower, checking to make sure everything was squeaky clean. I had gone out the night before and gotten my hole destroyed, so there was no telling how things were this morning. That went well and I grabbed lube, fresh poppers, and a towel. I opened up the motorhome and opened the driveway gate directly in front of it. Calling it a motorhome was a bit of an understatement. It is a converted coach and is really big and really unique. I'd been fucked in it once before when I was bringing it home from the auction I bought it at. This was the first time I'd tricked in my motorhome.

I waited inside the motorhome, lubed, naked, with my poppers open, ready to get fucked. This was a great way to start the morning I thought. Across the street the neighbors 20 something son was washing his car. He was hot in his own right and I stood there stroking myself wondering what sort of manhood was between his legs. He was a nicely built black man of average height.

My fantasy was quickly disrupted when the blue Toyota Corolla pulled in. It was a nice, basic car. A slim man stepped out and adjusted himself. He walked hesitantly up to the gate and then came around to the door. I could see all of this through the big window in the front of the motorhome. It was tinted with reflective film so I could see out, but nobody could see in.

He stepped in and said hi. He almost immmediately unbuttoned his pants and let them drop to his knees. Out flopped an absolutely beautiful cock. Somewhere between 8.5 and 9 and a little thicker than average with increasing thickness near the thick head. Probably one of the nicest cocks I'd had the pleasure of. I dropped to my knees and started sucking him hard. It took only a minute or two to get him fully erect. He had a gentle upward curve.

I assumed the position bent over the couch while he applied lube to his cock. He slipped in and it was surprisingly easy. I thought to myself that he had the perfect fucking cock. He wasted no time and begin banging my ass at a medium tempo. After a few minutes of mutual moaning I asked if I could ride him. He said sure and we switched positions.

I climbed on top of him and eased myself down onto his cock, steadying myself with my hands on his broad shoulders. My rock hard cock was precumming on his smooth midsection as I bounced on his lap and worked my hole in and out over his cock. We were both enjoying the hell out of each other. I put his hands on my shoulders and neck to see what sort of play he was into. He took the bait and started to fuck me more forcefully. After a minute he pulled me into him and held me there. I nuzzled him and we started making out a bit. Then I held his shoulders as I leaned back with his cock fully in me. Again I started to ride him and then stopped after a few seconds.

He was getting more aggressive. He told me to lay face down on the couch and he would bang me from behind. The furniture dimensions were nearly perfect for this. As I got off of him I spotted some white fluid that had leaked out of my ass and onto his belly. I teased and asked if he had cum once. He said maybe a little, but that he wasn't done with me at all. That was hot, I rarely made guys cum by riding them.

He got behind me and slipped into me burying his meat all the way inside me until he slammed his hips against my ass. He then started pile driving my hole. It was hurting a little bit and there was no way I could grab my poppers. I had put them on the window ledge which turned out to be convenient as I could just manage to inhale from them. He kept on banging me and telling me how good that ass was. He was making my hole sore and I started squeezing my ass around his cock as he pushed.

This must have sent him over the edge. He leaned over me

and started fucking alot harder. This was amazing sex, but getting better. He said to me, "You want my load whore?" "Yes Sir" I replied. "good, you are going to get it." he said and with that he slammed into me and I felt his meat pump a load of seed inside my hole.

He held his cock inside me and the throbbing subsided. He slowly pulled out while telling me, "I want to make sure my load stays in there. That's my hole now." I was totally turned on by this stud. We made small talk as he cleaned up and got dressed. I asked him, "So are you single or stray?" "Stray, open marriage." he said. "How often do you want to fuck this ass?" I asked. "When I can get free," He said as he turned and walked out.

Riding Horsecock

The maze area was very crowded. My eyes hadn't adjusted but I could tell there were 6 to 8 people in the play area of the maze at Midtown Spa. This was my favorite bathhouse in Houston. A touch sleazy but not pretentious. From what I could tell there were 3 bottoms on the mattress and at least 3 tops fucking ass or playing with it. The one closest to me was a 6'2" black guy and he was hot. As my eyes adjusted I could see the black guy near me was probably 10 inches. He began fucking the guy laying closest to me and was really pile driving that ass.

A man was exiting and made his way through the crowd and stopping past me. He was nicely build, 5'10 and middle aged. I couldn't really see anything in his towel as he walked past. He stopped a few steps past me and walked back. I was standing with my towel in my hand and my naked, lubed ass exposed. He stopped directly behind me and rubbed his bulge against me. He was big…. very big. He pushed against me and began to grind my ass with his package. I leaned back and asked if he wanted to fuck here or in my room. "Your room" came the reply. I replied, "406, see you there."

I was rock hard, and horned up as hell. I walked to my room and he was right behind me. He walked in behind me and shut the door, dropping his towel and throwing it in the corner. His cock flopped out. It was huge! I swear I had seen this dick before and had it. It was the largest cock I'd ever had. It was not the right first, cock for the day as he was easily 10 by 7. Meaning he was 10 long and 7 around. I told him to hang on while i opened fresh poppers. I was going to need that to take him.

I opened my poppers and lubed him good several times and my hole good before bending over to submit to his will. He wasted no time putting the head of his dick against my ass. It was pitch black in my room except for the light coming in over the wall. He pushed but my hole was not opening. He didn't let this stop him and simply pushed harder, forcing my hole to open wide for him. He slid all the way in despite my moaning and protests between inhaling poppers as deeply as I could. He slowly pulled out and then thrust back in while holding my ass still. He picked up the rythm and was pounding my hole while periodically slapping my ass. I had my head against the wall and was desperately inhaling poppers hoping for relief from the force that was violating my ass. On the one hand it hurt in a very special way, and on the other hand it was a huge turn on being forcefully used by this man and his cock. If ever I had seen a monster cock or donkey dick, this was it! He just kept pounding my hole, standing behind me and working me over. After about 30 minutes I told him I needed a break. He pulled out and let his cock hang there. I stood up, slightly dizzy from being fucked. He reminded me that he had fucked me before and that it was good to see me again. I thanked him and told him to use me again in a bit.

He walked out and I sat there trying to figure out the state of my insides. After a few minutes I grabbed my towel and walked down to the maze area. It was mostly empty again so I laid my towel on the play area and bent over. An older guy with an 8 inch cock walked up behind me and slipped his cock in. He pumped me for a few minutes before seeding my hole. While he was fucking my donkey cock trick walked up. When the older guy walked off donkey cock walked over and leaned over me. He growled, "I thought you needed a break?" Before I could reply he added, " I need some more ass and I'm taking it now." "Yes sir" I said. He slid in me much to the amazement of a couple of people who were watching by now. He proceeded to work up to pounding my ass. After a few minutes he just stopped pulled out and walked away, leaving me wondering what was wrong. He later came up and said he just wanted some variety.

A third guy had been watching and now walked up to play with my ass. He was latin with a scruffy beard and furry chest, probably early 30's. His cock had a pronounced downward curve. He lubed and up and slid in to what would be a marathon fuck. My ass was sore, so a curve down and a marathon fuck weren't exactly a great idea. After about 10 minutes he showed no sign of getting off and I let him slide out. I told him I had to piss and walked off before he could slip back in. The reality was he had been pumping my bladder and it wasn't terribly comfortable.

I walked off to the bathroom, but couldn't piss. I said hi to some friends and wandered back to see if I could get some more dick. It was getting late and I needed to go soon. Horse cock walked over to me and whispered in my ear that he needed to cum in some ass. I suggested my room and he agreed. He again wasted no time in my room, this time with the lights on. He positioned me bent over and forced his thick shaft inside me. He was fucking harder this time and I knew that he was on the path to seeding me. After 5 minutes or so he succeeded in getting off as I heard him moan and shove his cock deep into my ass. He unloaded and then held it there for 30 seconds or so before slowly slipping back out. He thanked me and I thanked him for the cock. I suggested videoing my hole next time he fucked it. He laughed and walked out.

Night Pump

I had just come in from hanging out at the local adult theater. It was dead. There was this really super aggressive middle aged Latin cock sucker who kept pawing everyone. This is the kind of aggression that gets your ass kicked. No means NO! I had managed to score one load from a guy I hadn't seen in ages.

He started off with, "Hey, I've been to your house before." I looked at him, not recognizing him and said, "Oh, I suppose you want to fuck my ass?" He said, "Yes!" With that we both started looking for a booth that would lock and wasn't disgusting. After a couple of tries we wound up in the one I played in before. This time the TV wasn't working and it was pitch black. Just as well I thought to myself.

We both proceeded to strip down enough to fulfill our roles. I fumbled and knocked the lube over a couple of times before managing to get him and I both lubed up. I hit my poppers and bent over. It's funny how you can recognize a cock by feel, but I knew who he was. Not too big, not too small, a funny curve and a big head. Yup, I knew that dick.

He banged me for a few minutes and creamed my hole. Then asked me if I had any tissue paper or toilet paper. I was glad it was dark, he couldn't see the "why is that my problem" look on my face as I apologized and said no. We both got dressed and I let his load ooze out of my hole. He left and I resumed walking around hitting on the black guys. I wasn't having any luck and they were hitting on each other. I saw the hottest of them come out of the booth with the super aggressive Latin guy. Well, I thought, that explains why he was grabbing the guys dick… it must work enough.

It was almost midnight, I decided to leave. On my way out I stopped to read a notice posted on the wall about the police raiding the place. "Keep it zipped up so you don't get arrested." It read. I shook my head and walked out. A couple of Asian boys were sitting outside and they smiled at me as I jumped in my convertible and put the top down. It was a nice cool night and that was at least good for a drive home.

When I got home I was starving so I ate a cupcake and sat down at the computer. I logged on to BBRTS and A4A to see if I could find some dick. A guy I had been going back and forth with was online. I messaged him, "Want to breed ass?" We went back and forth and I agreed to come over right then and there. It was 1am now, but I was desparately horny and not ready for sleep. I had to be up at 8am but I didn't give a fuck. I managed to get to his place by 1:30 and parked. I walked up to the door and tapped lightly on it. He answered from behind the door, naked and invited me in. He was very slender, skinny, but had a huge 9 inch cock hanging out. He bounded up the stairs with his hard cock bouncing left and right. He told me to follow him.

I made my way up the stairs quickly and stopped at the top. He lived in a small 1 bedroom loft apartment. It was a nice layout, but very modestly furnished. A cross between broke student and I don't give a fuck single. I stripped at the top of the stairs and made a pile of my belongings. He was laying back on the bed touching his cock and I was getting hard.

I wasted no time lubing myself and opening my poppers. I brought a fresh bottle with me. He told me to suck him and I did. He made me suck his cock for 5 to 10 minutes, slurping up and down his shaft. He would periodically start pumping me while asking how I liked it. I kept my mouth shut, it was rude to talk with your mouth full, especially when it was full of cock.

Finally, he told me to lube him up and sit on it. I did as I was told, but hit my poppers hard first. He was thicker than I thought and it was long. I was sore from getting bred by the big monster cock the day before. He had done a number on my cock.

He was pushing my limits, but I enjoyed it. I rocked on him and he pushed himself inside me. We were both enjoying each other. Then the trash talk started. That made it hotter with various insults and threats mixed in for color. He told me to hold myself still above him, the head of his cock just barely in me. Then he started to bounce against the bed, thrusting himself in me with each rise. This went on for a while and he scolded me when I tried to sit on him. After about 20 minutes he grew tired of it and told me to lay down. He got behind me and slid in and started banging it. A slow steady fuck deeply stretching my hole. He showed no signs of cumming and so I told him I was getting sore. He said we could stop and he would just owe me a load later. We both agreed and we laid next to one another. I apologized for not being able to handle him and he said it was no problem. He had enjoyed fucking the load out of my hole. I smiled and we both laughed. I had not told him about the other guy's load, but he apparently felt it and didn't care.

Cream Filling Sandwich

It had been a late night last night, but I woke up at 8:45 and reached for my phone. I needed to see if work was on fire or not. I really wanted another 4 hours of sleep. I went to bed at 3:30am. Sigh. No issues at work, but Grindr and Text were on fire. The text was the most interesting. I had one from Ass Pounder. Hmm, I had been wanting this one since last week. It was just a hello, so I said hi back and went to Grindr to clear the 7 messages there.

Ass Pounder wanted to know if I was horny. I replied and said kitty was in heat. He asked if I could get up there. I said sure, but that I needed to shower real quick. I jumped up and went to piss and shower. I really needed to know if my ass was clean. Luck was on my side... it was clean. I checked my schedule and texted back that I was good to go. He said good and sent me a picture of a cock and asked if I wanted some of that too. I said sure and asked when. He said his friend wanted to join in and in about 40 minutes. Perfect I thought as I got ready and got dressed. He sent me the address and warned me to watch for no parking signs as his neighborhood was vicious about towing. I found a spot that had other cars parked there and was free from no parking signs. It took me a bit to find his place, but I did as I was told and let myself in. I walked to the 3rd floor. it was a really nice place.

He welcomed me and told me to strip down, so I did. He was laying back on the bed stroking his fabulous cock. I climbed on to the bed and started to suck him when I heard someone come in behind me. It was a short, well dressed white guy who was a bit older. He was hot I thought. I kept sucking and he wasted no time stripping down. What a way to start the morning I thought as I looked at the white guys 8" cock and slurped on the black guys 9.5" thick cock.

White boy walked over and stood by me while the black guy pushed me onto that white dick. I sucked him a bit and marveled at what a nice cock it was. I could see them making motions out of the corner of my eye but couldn't tell what they were agreeing to.

No matter, I would find out soon enough. The white guy pulled out and lubed himself up. He maneuvered to my ass and slid in all the way. Ass Pounder moved around and started using my mouth while white guy was pumping my ass. Ass Pounder said to him, "This is the one I was telling you about. He likes it hard and he can take a pounding." I stopped long enough to let out a "Meow" and we all three chuckled. I resumed servicing Ass Pounder's cock while White guy pumped my hole.

45

After a little while he blew his wad and rolled off my ass and over next to me. He was really sexy. Ass Pounder got up behind me and slipped in to my freshly creamed hole. I shifted a bit and put my head on White guy's chest. He put his arms around me and held me a bit. I was getting my hole worked by the black guy and almost cuddling with the white guy.

Ass Pounder stopped, he was having trouble staying hard. I think he was jealous. Just then my phone started ringing. I walked over to see what it was and picked it up to answr. It was my best friend. I looked at the two studs as I answered with, "Hey, I'm in the middle of something hot, can I call you back in a bit?" My bestie said sure and I hung up. They both looked at me and I explained it was my bestie and we all laughed.

I walked back over and was ready to resume. Ass Pounder put me on my back and legs in the air. White guy straddled me and put his cock in my mouth. I was getting dicked double at the same time. OMG this was hot. After a bit we stopped again.

We all moved to the edge of the bed. Ass pounder had me bent over and White guy was there for moral support. I pulled him in so I was between his legs, he was laying back in front of me and Ass pounder had my hole. I hinted that my fantasy had been to be held down and fucked. White guy was happy to oblige, holding me tightly while Ass pounder worked my hole and moved both of us with the force of his thrusts. I was really enjoying the white guy.

Ass Pounder was having trouble staying hard and White guy had to go. We all made small talk for a few and then white guy bolted. Ass Pounder only had 20 minutes til he had to work. I suggested we try and get him off. I kissed him and tried to build up his ego a bit. I sensed he was jealous of the white guy's chemistry with me. I couldn't deny it, I was genuinely attracted to the white guy. Nice cock, pretty smile, clipped chest…. filthy mind…. hmmm.

My attention paid off and Ass Pounder got nice and hard. He bent me over and started tearing my ass up again. It was hurting, but felt good. He was pumping me hard and making me moan loudly. Finally he managed to nut in my ass. That wasn't enough though as he worked it in. When he finished we chatted a bit and he gave me a tour before showing me out.

Deep Tissue Massage

The lobby always had that too clean appearance to it. It was accented by the sickeningly friendly woman at the counter. I could tell she was drinking the Kool-Aid. Hell she was probably fucking the manager. No big deal, I wasn't here for her or the bull shit new age nonsense for sale in the lobby. While I generally hated the pretense at Massage Envy, I did enjoy getting a massage. As I checked in I learned that my regular massage therapist wasn't available. He had called in sick so they had switched me to David. She hoped I didn't mind. Well fuck! I thought. I guess I was going to be fine with it.

I sank down in the chair and pulled out my iPhone to see what was lurking on Grindr. I was more horny than sore, but I had signed up for the massage a few days ago. Grindr was the same boring fucks that always wanted to trade pictures. It was like some sort of beginner porn or something. As I was scrolling through the prospects I heard my name being called, "John…." I looked up at the source of the voice.

I thought to myself, this must be David. I sure hope he can give a good massage. He wasn't that much to look at. Okay, he was flat fucking ugly. I reminded myself that I was hear for the rub down not the fuck down. I greeted the little troll at the door and smiled as politely as I could muster.

"Hi John, David was busy setting up the room from his last client and wanted me to bring you back. I'm Sam., he said. "Thank you Sam," I replied. Sam proceeded to escort me back to room 12. This room was usually colder than a Baptist preacher's wife. Sam motioned for me to go into the room, but stayed out of the room. Before closing the door he said, "David prefers that you be face down on the table if you want to make yourself comfortable. Enjoy your massage."

And with that Sam closed the door, leaving me in the dimly lit, freezing cold room listening to fake beach noises. This was unusual. Protocol was that the therapist greeted you and then wasted 10 minutes of your time while you got undressed. Whatever, I thought. It was late and they probably all wanted to get the fuck out of here. I resigned myself to be surprised and quickly got undressed and under the sheet on the table. To my pleasant surprise the table was warm. At least someone had something right I thought.

I settled in under the sheet, face down as requested and waited for David. After a few minutes there was a gentle tap followed by the door opening. I glanced up as David introduced himself, "Hi John, I'm David." He continued, "I've read your chart and I'm ready

47

to give you a good working over." Ha! I thought, you hardly know the working over I want boy! David was 25, 5'9" probably 180# a bit on the stocky/muscular side. He was clean cut with short hair and was lightly tanned. In a word this guy was hot. I would enjoy the massage for sure, but I wanted more. "Great," I replied.

David placed his hand on my back and walked around me. Therapists had this pattern of 'grounding' on the patient. I could tell alot from touch and David's hand wasn't the cold, disinterested one. I decided I would be chatty with him. Sometimes I was dead quiet and just laid there enjoying my massage. Othertimes I was chatty and would have a good conversation with the therapist. My only rule was that they didn't unload all their personal problems on me.

I started out with the standard fare, "How long have you been doing bodywork?" "About 5 years," he replied as he began to work my shoulders. He was definitely good. He ran his muscular hands down my back and I was acutely aware of his crotch very close to my head. I could smell his sweaty crotch! It smelled delicious. David's hands were working my sore back and finding knots while my mind was in the gutter. He worked his way progressively down my back pausing for a second at my ass. As he begin to massage my ass he remarked, "You have a nice ass, very firm and muscular." "Thanks, I hear that alot," I replied as I smiled and laughed a bit. He didn't skip a beat and replied, "I bet." Hmmm I thought, if only you knew. It was pretty unusual to have the therapist massage my ass, but it had happened before and was pretty inoccuous. I had made sure to be squeaky clean before coming in. That was my habit.

He worked his way down my legs to my feet as we traded small talk. He had moved to Houston from Raleigh, North Carolina. That explained the wholesome look and friendly demeanor. He had me turn over and massaged my legs and chest and neck. This was normally where things wound down with some pitiful plea for a tip and another massage.

Instead David told me to turn over again. Sure, I thought. I glanced at the clock as I turned over and realized we had run over by about 20 minutes. I kept my mouth shut and hoped I wasn't going to get billed extra. He said, "You had some extra tension in your back that I want to take care of." "Thanks I said," as I thought to myself that the real tension was in my ass. He lowered the table down to where I was about 10 inches off the ground. Massage Envy had some great powered tables, which was one of their redeeming qualities. David straddled me and removed the draping so he could get to my back. This was unusual for sure. He began to work my lower back and slid down to my ass. He settled down on to my legs which was my first clue that this was about to get interesting. As

48

he lowered himself he said, "You don't mind if I touch you do you?" "Not at all, touch whatever you want," I replied. "I will," he said. He started to work his way up my back, leaning forward as he did. I could feel a bulge in his pants and knew that he was turned on. That was hot I thought to myself, but it probably wouldn't go anywhere.

As if I to ensure I hadn't imagined his cock pushing against my ass he paused to adjust himself. After which he remarked, "I've got a little tension myself that needs releasing." I thought for a second before replying, "I'd be happy to help." As if on queue he stood up and unbuckled his pants. I didn't dare turn around, but I could tell he was taking his pants off. He said in a low voice, "I had hoped you might." Before I could reply he was back on top of me, skin against skin this time. He said, "I have some lube here which will feel better than massage lotion, but I'm a bit aggressive when I fuck." As he said this he was lubing himself and my hole. I replied, "bring it!" He was probably 8.5 and a bit thicker than average from what I could feel. I hadn't turned around to look lest I spoil the moment.

He wasted no time and deftly moved back to position the head of his cock against my ass. He leaned over me and whispered, "Let me in or I'll break down your hole." Hot I thought as he eased into my hole. I desperately wanted some poppers. He must have been reading my mind because I heard the unmistakeable sound of a cap being removed and him inhaling. He handed the bottle to me and I happily took it.

He wasn't messing around and started pumping my hole. He was very good at being a top and I had been craving his cock the whole time he had been massaging me. As he was fucking me I wondered about the time and if we were going to get interrupted. This was somewhat risky for both of us and the last thing I needed was drama. David plowed my hole good and deep for a few minutes before unloading in me. He hadn't lasted long and he knew it. He bit gently on my ear and said, "That's a sample. I'll give you my number for later." "Deal sir," I replied. He pulled out and cleaned up and got dressed. He leaned over and whispered to me, "You'll leave me a $5 tip." I thought that was odd, but before I could respond he said. "You normally tip $15 according to the computer. So $5 will make them think you didn't like my massage. I'm headed to the front to tell them you complained which is why we ran over." We both smiled as he walked out the door. His seed was deep in my hole and oozing a bit as I got up and got dressed. I pulled myself together and headed to the front.

When I got to the front the manager was the only one there and he was clearly ready to get the fuck out. He asked how my massage was. "It was okay, but I don't think we should schedule him again." He looked up and replied, "Most people request repeats with David." I replied, "I didn't care for his technique, but I can see why others might." He smiled, "Okay, I'll take him off your list."

As I signed the card receipt and put in the tip I noticed that the manager's phone was sitting there, unlocked. He had Grindr up. Hmm, I thought to myself. It made for an interesting moment because I think he realized I saw his phone. He grabbed it at the first moment and locked the screen. He smiled and said, "Have a nice night John." I smiled back and said, "I did, thanks." He had a twinkle in his eye so I knew there was more going on when he replied, "I'll see you next time."

French Connection

I had just finished Nude Yoga at Club Houston and was walking upstairs to my room. We made contact and locked eyes for a moment. He had beautiful eyes and a really furry chest. My heart practically skipped a beat, he was blond, clean cut, and had a super furry chest without being a gorilla. He had to be 30 something. No way in hell he was actually interested in me I thought. I kept walking up and smiled briefly back at him as he turned the corner. I dropped my yoga mat in my room, had a refreshing drink of Coca-Cola and sat for a moment relaxing.

I was hornier than a stray cat in heat so I lubed my hole, grabbed my lube, poppers, and towel and headed out to prowl for some dick. I made a lap of the rooms and glanced at the guys in their rooms stroking their dicks and watching twink-porn. I decided to head to the dark maze play area and see who was in there. Other than a few aggressive Gaysian boys slamming booth doors there wasn't much going on. I walked back to the cocksucking catwalk area and leaned on the wall in the dimly lit area. The play area has a horshoe shaped raised platform that guys can stand on and other guys can walk up and suck them off through glory holes. It's a nice setup for sucking dick, but I usually want more than that.

As I was standing there my furry stud walked in. We made eye contact again as he walked up the stairs and leaned against a wall across from me. I considered pinching myself to see if it was real and then gathered my courage and pride and walked over to where he was standing. He wasted no time in pulling his towel back and stuffing a thick 7.5" cut cock into my mouth. I slowly serviced his cock, letting it glide in and out of my mouth and feeling every bump, every vein, and every groove on his manhood. We alternated with him working my mouth and me bobbing my head on his cock. I was really into this guy and working his dick good. I could hear the occassional moan and knew he was enjoying it. I raised my hands and put them on the ledge next to him as it made it easier for me to float on and off his rod. He reciprocated and lowered his hands to play with my hair. This was probably the most sensual blow job I had given in ages. It was really wonderful, but my ass was twitching and wanting way more. I could also sense that a crowd was gathering and the only thing I hate worse than a little dick is a cock blocking queen trying to interfere with my trick.

My stud seemed to be thinking the same thing. He paused me and lifted my chin up so we made eye contact. He said in very accented English, "Let's go to my room." I felt like I'd won the lottery as I replied, "Sure!"

51

I followed him to room 242 and he opened the door. As I followed him in he shut the door behind me and it was just the two of us. He was nicely built, super furry, and absolutely handsome. He reached over and pulled me to him and we started making out. I was stroking his cock with my hand and dropped to my knees to suck him some more. He let me go for a few and then stopped me and pulled me up to him and asked in his thick accent, "Do you want to fuck?" "Yes!," was my enthusiastic reply. He laid back and slipped a condom on his beautiful cock. I hate condoms, but I wanted this man inside me and was willing to tolerate the condom. I knew it would tear my ass up and hurt later, but I didn't care right now.

I positioned myself over him and we made out for a few minutes. I asked him his name and he said it was Marc. I asked him where he was from, "France," came the shocker. Normally French guys hadn't been that hot... I guess they just keep the ultra hot ones there. This guy was a 12 on a scale of 1 to 10. Aside from being handsome and hung he was really taking time to make sure I was having fun. Kissing was turning us both on. I lubed him up and fingered my hole a bit with lube to make the best of it. Then I slowly pushed my ass down around his thick blond cock. I could feel him pulse as I lowered my tight hole around him. He moaned as I started to rock slowly up and down on his shaft. I would periodically lean down to make out with him which gave him the opportunity to thrust up into me.

After a few minutes we switched up the positions and tried a few before settling on what I call "doormat." It's where I lay flat on my stomach and the guy gets behind me. Normally guys will pile drive my ass in this position. Marc was very different and kept making out with me and taking his time. It was the kind of sex I dream about having in a relationship, but which always seems to elude me in my relationships.

After about 20 minutes of intense passionate sex I told him I wanted his load. He repeated the question to me, "You want my cum?" "Yes please," I replied. He thrust into me and paused while making out with me. Then he pulled out and reached his hand down and removed the condom. I saw it last as he flung it on the floor and then he slipped back inside me and what was already fantastic sex got even more passionate as he was truly inside me. He pounded me hard for a few minutes before tensing up and moaning as he blew his load deep inside me. He just laid there with his chin on my shoulder nuzzling against the side of my head. It was really amazing sex. He slowly slid out and then I rolled over as he laid back down on my chest. I was running my fingers through his hair and stroking his neck gently. He was overnighting and headed back the next morning. He worked for Air France as a pilot.   We laid there and chatted for a few minutes before we each had to go back to our worlds. I thanked him and told him to have a safe trip before I walked out the door and back to my room.

Action Scene

Sometimes the planets align and my schedule clears like the clouds on a dark night. Tuesday was one of those days where I had some time off of work and was able to get to Club Houston early. Tuesdays are half-price rooms. All the regular rooms were gone when I arrived, as was the sling room and the "mirror" room. I settled for a video room and hurried upstairs. I got undressed and made my way to the maze. It was busy, but mostly with busy bodies. I was not having any luck and 4:30 turned into 8:30. All I had to show for it was a hot black guy, Gorilla Guy, I had talked into fucking me in my room. He pulled out and shot on my stomach which was quite the waste. He had wanted to fuck with a condom and finally relented to bareback after I told him no for the 400th time. He had a nice, thick cock, but came pretty quickly.

I wandered back to the maze again as 8:30 became 9 pm. I couldn't believe how slow it was. They usually sell out of rooms and that hadn't happened tonight. There were a few guys I wanted but none were biting. I was beginning to think about going to dinner and just chalking it up to a bad night. The only amusing thing so far had been a jack off show between a couple of overbuilt white guys and a black guy I call King Kong. King Kong has what looks like a 12 inch dick and the attitude to go with it. He rarely gives me the time of day…. which is fine. I like a challenge, not a suicide mission. I walked around the corner to the cocksuck catwalk and found the two muscle bumpkins jacking off with king kong and a few wannabes watching and trying to get in the mix. Visor boy, this otherwise hot Latino with a bad attitude was right there in the mix. He had a nice looking cock, but it was undone by his unpleasant attitude.

I decided to go stand by the booths, which was probably a stroke of good fortune. I noticed this average furry cub eyeing me from across the dark play area. He was mostly hard and stroking his cock. Suddenly he vanished from view. I couldn't tell what booth he went into, so I just stayed put. About a minute later he came around to my side and went into the booth closest to me. I went into the booth next to him and immediately set to work sucking his cock. It was a nice average cock, but he was aggressively working my mouth with it. I wasted no time in lubing myself and him and then sitting on that cock and letting him pound my ass. Ordinarily this would constitute a pretty good night….but it was about to get alot better. He stopped fucking me and walked out of his booth. He rattled my door as I gathered my things. When I opened it to leave he pushed me back and came into the booth with me. I offered that we could go to my room and he replied gruffly, "no I'm fucking you here." Hot! I thought as he spun me around and stuffed his cock in

54

my ass. It took me a few seconds to get a workable position during which he was still banging me causing me to bump my head a bit. Nothing like good rough sex. I was vaguely aware of others in adjoining booths watching, but I didn't really give a shit. After about 5 minutes the loudspeaker came on announcing that it was time to clean the maze area. I suggested we could move to my room before the lights came on. He agreed.

We had no sooner walked out of the booth then the lights came on and everyone scattered in the maze area like cats running from a water hose. I confidently strode ahead to my room only occassionally glancing back to make sure he was there.

When we arrived I shut the door behind him and started to make out with him while riding his cock. He had a bit of a belly, which was hot, but it makes the mechanics of riding an average cock and trying to make out difficult. I suggested that we switch positions so he could pound my ass. He asked if we could open the door and I said no... I envisioned a bunch of trolls watching and reaching in. He shrugged and bent me over, banging my ass good. Normally when I'm getting fucked like this I start moaning and tonight was no exception. After a few minutes I told him to open the door and see what he could find to join him. He smiled and said okay as he opened the door. I swear it hadn't been 3 minutes when I glanced back and noticed a crowd outside the door watching me get pounded. I smiled and laughed to myself as I asked him if he had found any dick yet to join him. Not yet he replied, but it's looking good.

There were probably 5 guys crowded around the door to my room watching cubstud pound my ass. Most of them had their cocks out and I would occassionally motion to them to come in, but none were up for it. One was stroking his cock through his towel, visor guy. It's kind of annoying for someone to want to watch a scene, but hide their cock.... so I loudly said something about timid bitches hiding their cocks and slammed the door. Cubstud laughed and kept pounding my ass. After about 2 minutes I opened the door expecting the crowd would be gone. To my surprise Visorguy was leaving and everyone else had stayed put.

This time a second guy came in, and was playing with his cock, but not wiling to fuck despite requests from me and cubstud. He finally strolled off and a younger cub came in. He had a more pronounced belly, but a slightly bigger cock to go with it. He was a bit cuter, but both cubs were totally fuckable. Youngcub swapped off with cubstud and started drilling my ass. Cubstud got on my bed and layed down in front of me playing with me and himself as he watched youngcub pound my hole. I noticed some motion out of the corner of my eye and realized that the floor guy was changing the room across the hall. I could see him sneaking glances at the orgy going on in my room. I wondered for a second if he would get hard, tell us to stop and close the door, or just ignore it. A few seconds later the other young floor guy drifted by. He stopped for a second and watched the action before going back to whatever he was supposed to do. Youngcub finally came after about 10 minutes and shot a huge load in my ass. I stood up and leaned back to thank him and we kissed for a few minutes. As he walked away I turned my attention back to cubstud who said he needed a break. That was fine with me, my knees hurt and my ass was sore.

I used my towel to mop up all the lube that had spilled and put my lube bottle backtogether. Someone had apparently ripped the flip top apart trying to get it open. lol. Silly boys. I took a nice shower and decided it was time to go swim a few laps.

The pool was nice and warm, and I wound up talking to a couple of hot hung black guys. One, Tall Guy, had a room across from mine and had seen my little scene. Tall guy wandered off and Gorilla Guy came over and sat down. Scuba dude (the other black guy) wandered off and it was just me and Gorilla Guy chatting. He asked me what undetectable meant and so we talked about safer sex for a few minutes. I figured that was that. He looked at me with a twinkle in his eye and said, "you wanna go upstairs again?" Sure I said and jumped out of the pool. I quickly dried off and we went upstairs to my room.

We made out a little bit with the door closed and he again offered to use a condom, to which I said no several times. I thought he was gonna give up and then he put me on my back with my legs up and started to fuck me. He didn't quite have enough lube in but I didn't really care. After a second he pulled his cock out and looked down. I thought for a second maybe I had gotten dirty, so I asked if everything was okay. He had this horrified look on his face as he asked me, "Is that cum?" I looked down at his cock and realized he had pulled Youngcub's load out of my ass. I chuckled, relieved it was not shit, and said "yea looks like it." This was apparently too much for him so he excused himself and took off.

I decided to go back to the maze and see what I could find. I ran into MaybeStud in the video porn area. He looked vaguely familiar from somewhere, but I couldn't figure out where. I stood there jacking off and he was jacking off. I couldn't quite tell what he wanted and then Gorilla Guy walked up to me again. I heard some noise outside the video room and realized an orgy had spontaneously formed outside the video room. I watched it with Gorilla Guy as I whispered that we should hook up at my house sometime and I'd make sure it was just his load in my ass. He was game for it he said.

When the orgy wound down I wandered back and MaybeGuy was still sitting there stroking. I took a seat next to him and he said he was a top and that he wanted to fuck me raw. Sure I replied. Before we could act, CubStud showed up and sat down next to me….. and started playing with me.

Somehow we all agreed to go back to my room. It was pretty obvious another round of show n blow would be going on so we left the door open. I was sucking Maybestud while Cubstud fucked me. MaybeStud was having trouble getting hard and Cubstud was banging my ass. Maybestud excused himself to go get a cockring. Just when we had about given up on him he showed back up and plopped down next to me. I was playing with him a bit but Cubstud was really drilling me. A tall white guy walked in and started suck-ing Maybestud. Maybestud was wide eyed looking at me and the newcomer and me again. I thought it was kind of ballsy to just drop in but what the hell. I reached over to newcomer and he had a big thick cock, so I started to stroke it in hopes that he would breed me. As he started to get hard he made it obvious he wasn't interested in me. I laughed as I said, "Ok you can leave my room. Out you go" and with that gently pushed him up and out. Cubstud kept drilling me and finally managed to blow a load. Maybestud was still having trouble getting hard so we all agreed to take a break.

I mopped up my floor again and swapped out my towel. When I went to the shower I had a nice chat with NOLAguy, a hung black guy from New Orleans. I invited him to breed my ass next time he saw me. He smiled and said sure. As I walked out of the shower I saw Maybeguy so I asked him if everything was okay. He said sure and told me to come to his room. I smiled as I walked by his room. I needed my lube and poppers. By the time I walked back the door was closing and someone had scooped me. ☐ I decided this was a good time to pack up and head home. My ass was sore and I had at least 2 loads in my hole. As I walked by he told me I could at least get his name and number. The door was open again and I guess the other guy hadn't worked out. I looked at him and smiled and said "I'd like your cock and seed, can I still get that?" He laughed and said, "Sure." I quickly went back to my room and tossed the sheets and towel on the bed. I stripped and grabbed my lube and poppers and went back to his room. He bent me over and proceeded to drill my ass. He was probably an average size and not particularly thick, but it felt nice and he was pretty aggressive. After about 10 minutes he tensed up, moaned and shot his seed deep in-side me. I thanked him for his load and we exchanged numbers.

I went back to my room and got dressed. I gathered my things and headed down to the counter to checkout. When I got there the counter guy was smiling at me and asked "Well, did you have a good time?" I laughed and asked him, "Did you hear about my action scene or something?" He smiled and said, "Of course!"

Ownership Has It's Privileges

It was a typical Friday at Club Houston. I had managed to get there around 7:30 and taken advantage of happier-hours when rooms are half-off. I was standing upstairs in the glass windows looking down into the shower area. King Kong was stroking his soapy cock and teasing the guys. I was watching King Kong, this 6'2 built black guy with a 11"+ cock and trying to figure out which twink he was going to split in half. I thought to myself that it might be too big for me. As I was in my own world thinking about King Kong I heard a deep voice next to me say, "That's a nice ass you have." I snapped out of my thoughts and looked over to find a tall slender 30 something black guy in tight speedos standing next to me. "Thank you," I replied to him. I took inventory of him and wasn't terribly impressed. There was no bulge to think of and I figured he was one of those tragic men with a fine body and no cock to speak of. On the other hand it was slow and dreaming was about all I was going to get from King Kong. I guess he could tell what I was thinking because he put one hand on my ass. He squeezed gently as he leaned over and said, "Wanna come back to my room?" I looked at him and said, "Are you a top? Do you like to fuck raw?" He leaned closer and growled in my ear, "Come to my room and I'll bury seed in your ass." I really liked direct guys I thought to myself as I said, "Sure!"

I followed my new stud back to his room and he shut the door behind me. Black guys were generally down to business so I tossed my keys and towel by the door and proceeded to get down on my knees. He slipped his blue speedos off and threw them in the other direction. What emerged from his speedos was much much larger than I had anticipated. My hole spasm in anticipation wasn't entirely unexpected. He was slightly curved, thicker than average, maybe 1.75" across, and around 8 and 3/4 to 9 inches. Just what Dr. Kitty ordered I thought to myself. I pursed my lips and got his shaft wet before taking him in my mouth and working his cock good. A good top will always show some tendency to thrust if you are sucking him right. He wasted no time in putting his big soft hands behind my head and pushing his cock down my throat. He was considerate not to choke me, but I could tell he was going to be in control while we had sex. Fine with me I thought…. I need my hole used. After a few minutes of being throat fucked and struggling to take it I stood up and told him I had somewhere better to put his cock. I told him I would need to sit on it and he leaned back on the bed. I lubed him up good and then lubed my hole and hit my poppers hard before easing down onto his manhood.

He was big, but not unmanageable. Just the right size to stretch me out without tearing me up. He was also somewhat firm but sensuous. I began to ride his cock in an effort to relax my hole and he was tweaking my nipples. He pulled me down and kissed me before telling me that I could get on all fours or he would put me there and use my ass.

I really try to please as a bottom, so I got on all fours as I felt him slide into me from behind. He slid in all the way and then started pounding me before pushing me flat on to the bed. He thrust in and shuddered, pausing for a second before continuing to pound me. I didn't think anything of it. After about 20 minutes of pounding he put his arm over my shoulder and asked if I was enjoying myself.

"Of course," I replied. He put his head up against the back of my neck and growled that my hole was his as he shot his load in me.

Normally this is the end of the story for most black guys. It's just a nut and once they get it they are done and you are out. Not this one. He lay there with his cock inside me throbbing and his arm over me with his head pressed against the side of mine. I asked his name to which he replied, "Jacob." "Nice to meet you Jacob," I said. He squeezed me and said, "It's sir to you when my cock is inside you." "Nice to meet you sir," I replied. "Good boy," he said in my ear gently licking it. I moaned as he licked me and nibbled on my ears.

My moaning was turning him on and I felt him getting harder again. He quietly said in my ear, "I came twice when I was fucking you earlier, but I am going to put a 3rd load in. Your hole is mine." "Yes sir," I replied. I partially twisted around and gave him a deep kiss as he resumed penetrating thrusts into my ass. As his thrusts grew harder and more frequent I assumed a more passive position. He kept nibbling me which I very much enjoyed. I could tell after about 15 minutes he was getting closer. He growled in my ear, "This ass is mine." I replied, "yes sir." A few more thrusts and he shot another huge load in my ass. Absolutely fucking fantastic, I thought. He lay there with his cock inside me and muttered, "I'm holding my cock in so that my seed doesn't leak out. It's my claim to your hole." Hot I thought…. He told me, "I'm going to fuck you next week, give me your number." I had thoroughly enjoyed his cock so I gave him my number. True to form he texted me the next day and told me to be ready Saturday night to take care of him. We texted back and forth and he said, "I own that hole and ownership has it's privileges…. like using your ass to unload whenever I need it." "Yes it does," I texted back.

Stranded Stray

He could see the delivery truck making it's way down the street. Blake shook his head and thought, "What the fuck are they doing out in this?" He looked again, and the FedEx truck was trundling down the street. It was pushing water up into yards with it's wake. It reminded Blake of a ship in the ocean. An ocean was a fitting comparison to how much water had fallen in Houston. Hard, pounding, tropical rain with drops that seem the size of grapes. Each one thudding on the roof individually, but in unison creating a dull roar. He continued to watch the truck as it turned the corner and stopped in front of the house. It seemed like all FedEx drivers specialized in destroying transmissions and brakes. Even in 10+ inches of water this one had managed to skid the tires and grind the gears. Blake shook his head quietly as he watched the driver in the cab of the truck. Blake didn't remember ordering anything, but he often forgot about his Amazon Prime purchases before they arrived. That was half the fun of ordering online he thought to himself. As an added bonus he was going to get to watch some FedEx guy get soaked bringing whatever it was to the house. Hopefully he would keep the package dry at least!

He could tell that it was a white guy, but he couldn't see much through the rain and the truck windows. The door opened and a 4 foot wide blue, white, and orange umbrella emerged in a futile attempt to hold back the rain. Blake chuckled, this was going to be amusing he thought. "Yum," he said aloud as the driver emerged with the package in one hand and the umbrella in the other. He was around 32, 6 foot, nice build, short buzzed blond hair and damp. In fact he was getting wetter with each step. The umbrella seemed to pose a personal challenge to the rain as it swirled around the umbrella and landed on the poor driver.

As Blake walked to the door to open it he heard a "motherfucker..." from the front yard and arrived just in time to see the hot FedEx guy on his hands and knees in the water. Water play not withstanding, he guessed correctly that he had tripped on the sidewalk. The driver finally made it to the door and Blake opened the door before he could ring the bell. "Hi," Blake said. "Oh, Hi" the driver replied. His nametag indicated that he might answer to Alex on better days. Before Alex could say anything Blake offered, "So I guess you found the crack in the sidewalk? Yea sorry about that." Alex smiled and said "Yea, not exactly my favorite crack to find, but I'll live." Blake thought that was odd, but kept it polite, "Can I get you a towel to dry off with while I sign for the package?" "Sure," Alex said as he noticed the handsome guy who seemed to live here. "Come on in", Blake motioned, "Shut the door behind you so we don't float away, I'll be right back with a towel." Blake figured this would be one of those good deed's that replenish your balance at the Bank of Karma. Blake grabbed a couple of warm towels from the dryer and returned to the entryway where the hot FedEx guy was. By now a small puddle had drained down. Alex was looking like a big puppy who had come in from playing in the mud, only much much hotter. Blake signed for the package and invited Alex to dry himself off. Alex smiled and remarked, "I really appreciate the towel. This is a heck of a downpour and I don't think I can get back out of the neighborhood on Richmond Ave, is there another way out?" Blake laughed and said, "Yes, by airplane. Not until the water goes down a bit." Alex looked a little stressed at that and replied, "Ok" He pulled a phone out of his pocket which had somehow managed to avoid being drown and fiddled with it. "Texting home base letting them know I'm stuck until the water drains," he told Blake.

Blake decided there might be more to this opportunity than a box of whatever from Amazon. "Would you like to shower off and I'll throw your uniform in the dryer while we wait for the water to go down?" he asked Alex. Alex paused for a second and said, "I would want to put you out, but if you and your wife don't mind, yes" "Wife?" Blake replied. "Surely a nice guy like you has a wife in a wonderful house like this," Alex backpedaled. Blake laughed as Alex looked like a puppy with a mouthful of catshit caught in the litterbox. "I'm single and gay, is that alright?" Blake asked. "Absolutely" Alex replied with a smile and added, "I am too." Blake was a little surprised but took it in stride.

Alex noticed Blake do a doubletake and wondered if he was a bottom. Rain made him particularly horny and he would love to bust a nut in that ass he thought to himself. Of course this was risky as it was strictly against FedEx policy to fuck a customer. Only customer service had this pleasure.

Blake led Alex down the hall to the master bedroom and instructed Alex to make himself comfortable. "Put your wet clothes in a pile and I'll get them in the dryer for you while you are in the shower. I'll throw a t-shirt and pair of shorts out for you while we wait, does that work?" Blake asked "Sure" Alex said as he pulled his shirt off to reveal a nicely toned body with plenty of clipped fur. Blake had intended to leave, but Alex didn't seem to care. Alex removed his belt and set it on the chair with his keys, phone, and wallet. He then glanced at Blake who was trying desparately not to stare as he unbuttoned his shorts and dropped them to the floor. Blake realized his own cock was probably beginning to show at about the same time Alex remarked, "I hope you don't mind, I've never been very shy." "No not at all, you have a nice body," Blake said as he glanced at Alex's physique and cock. He thought to himself that he must have a 8 inch cock with some nice thickness. It was soft, but Blake had seen enough dicks in his day to be able to guess accurately most of the time how big they were. By now Blake had a full on hard on that was hard to hide, so he adjusted it and apologized, "Sorry about that, it has a mind of it's own sometimes," he said. Alex laughed and replied, "Don't they all?" He continued, "I guess you have a pretty high sex drive too?" "Yes," Blake admitted while smiling. Alex replied, "The rain always gets me horny." Blake laughed, and replied, "Breathing makes me horny." Before Alex could reply Blake said the shower is in there on the left, I'll get your clothes started. He swore Alex's cock had grown a little, but this was awkward and hot so he didn't wanna stare outright.

Alex walked into the bathroom, it was very nicely done in slate and glass. It was probably the biggest walk in shower he'd ever seen in a home. He thought for sure that Blake must be a top too as he had gotten a woody when Alex undressed. He turned his attention to getting into the shower, finding the soap and getting the water going. As if on queue, Blake hollered to him, " It takes a few seconds for the hot water to get to the shower."

Blake scooped up the wet clothes and took them to the laundry room as the sound of running water from the bathroom echoed. It was odd to hear someone else in the shower, he thought. He no sooner had gotten the dials and buttons set on that damn Maytag dryer when he heard Alex calling his name.

"Blake?" Alex hollered out. "Yea? be right there..." Blake yelled back. The house wasn't very big and when he stuck his head in the bathroom he knew instantly what the problem was. Alex was standing half way across the shower with a puzzled look on his face. Before he could say anything Blake calmly said, "The second knob turns the hose off and turns on the shower head." "Oh," Alex replied, adding, "Thanks. Hey what is that hose for? cleaning the walls?" Alex had never seen a shower setup like this. It looked like an ordinary shower, but it was big enough for 2 or more guys and had two controls. On one wall was a second knob and a hose with a long black attachment. Blake smiled, it was his turn to be a little catty, he replied, "Yea the walls of my ass. I'm a bottom, sorry that's how bottom's get clean and I wasn't expecting company today so it's where I left it earlier, before all this damn rain started." Alex smiled back and said "No problem, I'm a top so I've never seen something like that." Blake glanced down and noticed that Alex was mostly hard and mostly 9 inches long and about 4.5 inches wide. "Sure thing, let me know if you need help with anything else," Blake offered.

You could have cut the silence with a knife that followed. Alex broke it though when he replied, "Yea there is someting..." Blake looked up and replied, "What's that?" "Well, you're a bottom, I'm a top....." Alex paused, "It's raining which makes me horny.... dude if you're up for it I need to bust a nut. You have a great looking ass...," Alex looked over to see if he'd blown it. He hadn't. Blake said, "I'd love to..... where do you want it? " "Right here works," Alex shot back. Blake stripped his t-shirt and shorts off and put them on the floor before grabbing his lube and poppers and jumping in the shower.

Alex hesitated and said, "You sure this is okay right?" "Totally, " Blake said as he dropped to his knees.   The water was bouncing off of him as he slid the door closed. He figured he would suck Alex a bit and lube his hole up at the same time. Alex had a perfectly shaped cock an the extra water from the shower made it really easy to slurp down on it until it hit the back of his throat. This made Alex pulse and get a little bit harder. Blake was sucking him as best he could while he tried to lube up his ass. Before Alex could say anything he started lubeing his cock while he was sucking it. Silicone lube was good for being water resistant and this was one of the reasons that was a good thing. Blake paused and asked, "You ready to fuck ass?" Without waiting for a response Blake stood up and took a hit of his poppers as he bent over. Alex didn't need a second invitation. He'd been wanting to get in this ass since he saw it earlier. He was throbbing and ready to plow. Alex put the head of his cock up against Blake's hole and just held it there.   He knew better than to just jam it in as that always made guy's spasm and clamp down. He could feel Blake pushing back against him and just as he was about to push forward Blake's hole opened up and took the head of his cock in. Hmm, that felt good, warm, moist. He heard Blake gasp a bit and smiled slyly as he liked it when guys moaned and protested a bit at his size. He'd been told he was bigger than some black guys. He slowly pushed in a little more knowing that he needed to get that hole open in order to enjoy it. Each time he pushed in Blake's ass opened up and let him in.

Blake was really enjoying this white meat. He was used to getting fucked by black guys so he could take dick, but this was still somewhat challenging.   It had been several days

After what seemed like an eternity Alex got his cock all the way inside Blake's hole. He leaned over his shoulder and growled in his ear, "You ready?" "Bring it," Blake replied back right away. Alex enjoyed the spunk as most guys were begging for more time at this point.   He pulled his throbbing cock out slowly, feeling Blake grip his cock and yet not try to crush it. Just before he popped out he reversed and slid all the way in, a little faster this time. That ass felt damn good on his cock. He paused again, no complaints. This time

64

he pulled it out and shoved it back in at more of a moderate tempo bottoming out with Blake's asscheeks pushing his thick blond bush away from his cock. He loved looking down at that. Still no complaints so he did it again and before he knew it, he was pounding that ass. Blake had both hands on the wall and his feet on either side of Alex bent at sort of a 45 degree angle.   Alex was pounding him full penetration bottoming out each time and it was making his balls burn with the desire to seed this ass and make it his. Alex asked out loud, "Do you want it?" Blake replied, "Yes Please!" Alex loved it when a bottom asked for his load. He pounded that ass a few more times before flooding it with his seed.

Blake stood there for a second enjoying the bliss of having just gotten this stud off and knowing his seed was deep in his gut. Before he could break the silence Alex slowly pulled out and then pulled him up and turned him around. They looked each other for a split second before Alex pulled him in and gave him a deep kiss and then said, "That was really nice, I need showers like this and ass like this more often." Blake smiled and said, "I would enjoy your cock again sometime, I'll give you my number when we dry off." "Ok," Alex replied. They both rinsed off and got out of the shower and toweled dry in the bedroom. Just as they finished Alex's work phone was ringing. They both looked at each other and smiled as Alex answered it completely naked. "I'm fine. Just talking with a friend and waiting the water out." He hung up and turned to Blake, "They wanted to make sure I was okay. Apparently another driver lost a truck in one of the creeks. They told us to stay put until the water level goes down," He said. Blake smiled and offered him his number to put in his personal phone. Alex accepted it and put on the shorts and t-shirt Blake had loaned him. His boner was still half hard and made a little tent in the shorts.

Silent Satisfaction

With a solid thud I hit the enter key, posting my ad to Craigstlist. This was back when Craigslist had a personals section, before the self-proclaimed righteous took over American government. It was my standard ass-up face down dark playspace fuck-ad. With any luck I'd get some dick. I walked off to the shower to get ready while Craig did his thing and found me some fun.

An hour or so later, with kitty fully cleaned out and ready to play, I checked my email to see what my ad had reeled in. A couple of trolls, a bottom asking if he could join me, and an email with a picture. I clicked to open the email and see what we had. Oh my, a very nice, thick 8" black cock. The body it was attached to was a little bigger than I liked, but the dick was very nice. I emailed back and asked when he wanted to play and what he was into. A few minutes later the response came back that he could come over in about 30 minutes, and he wanted no talking. None at all, just be completely dark and me on my knees. Hmm, okay, hopefully this would be fun I thought.

It was 11pm, so there was no problem keeping the garage dark. I had Frisky radio playing with some great dance music to set that bathhouse vibe. My tricks seemed to like that. I had my phone out and was watching my security cameras to see what showed up. If needed I could lock the door and run in the house. As if on queue a beat-up ass Toyota Corolla pulled into my driveway. It was loud enough that the neighbor was sure to know I had a visitor. Fortunately, I had remembered to turn off the motion lights in the driveway. Mr. Dick got out of his car and went over to the fence. I wondered what the fuck he was doing. Soon enough it became obvious he was pissing on the fence. Lovely. After he finished he headed over to the entrance to the play area. A little ghetto looking, like the car, but hopefully the goods would be as advertised.

He stepped in the entrance and paused. I broke protocol right away and told him to shut the outer door and then to open the inner door. He ignored me as if he hadn't heard me. Before I could repeat myself I heard the outer door close with a thud. I then heard him tug at the inner door and pull it open. I have a double door setup on the entrance to the play area. There is a lovely gloryhole there and it helps keep my play area private from my neighbors. As he had requested it was pitch fucking black in the play area. I could see very little, I'm sure he could see nothing. I had positioned myself on a furniture blanket near the entrance. Keeping quiet I reached out and felt his cock. He pulled it out and stepped towards my arm. At the same time his other hand reached out to find my head. As if he had done this a thousand times before he expertly slid his cock into my mouth and put his hands on the back of my head. He wasn't erect, but I could tell he had a nice tool. He slowly worked my mouth as the blood pumped into his cock and it grew. After a few minutes of fucking my mouth he was fully erect. It was a little thicker than I had expected, but a good 8 inches. I was happy to suck it so I quietly continued to service his cock. Feeling adventurous I ran my hands up the front of his torso and chest. Oh my, he was furry. Most black guys aren't furry, but he was furry enough to be a bear. A little belly to boot, but I didn't care, he had plenty of dick. He didn't object to my hands grazing his fur and nipples. I decided to tweak his nipples a bit and that elicited a moan before his hands moved mine further down. Okay, good to know where the limits are. He had a nice juicy cock and was beginning to ooze a little bit of precum. That was making my ass hungry. Maybe he could read my mind I thought. As if he could, he reached down and pushed me off his cock.

Before I could wonder what was going on he grabbed me by the ears and pulled me up. Not hard or rough, but he was deinitely in control. I guess his eyes had adjusted, because he seemed to know there was a fuck table nearby. No sooner had he stood me up then he pushed me to the table and bent me over. He spit in his hand a couple of times to lube up his cock and then pressed it against my ass. Without so much as a word he expertly slipped the head in my hole and tested it a couple of times before easing all the way in. I had no idea what to expect from him. Some guys get rough at this stage, but this guy seemed content to enjoy my hole. Slowly pumping in and out he started working my ass. Saying nothing, making no noises, and the one time I started to moan he pushed my head down and told me to be quiet. After about 20 minutes of this he pulled all the way out, waited about 3 seconds and then slipped all the way back in, balls deep. He proceeded to plunge fuck me for a little bit. I guess this was turning him on hard, because all of the sudden he stopped plunge fucking and started pounding my ass. It was as if he needed to punish me or take his frustrations out. He was fucking me hard, deep, and pinning me against the fuck table. I was biting a towel by now, trying to make zero noise as he used me like some sort of sex toy. I was wondering how much longer I could take him using me. I wouldn't have to wonder very long because all of the suddent he plunged in and stopped. I could feel him pulsing inside me as he unloaded his seed and moaned loudly. He stayed in me, motionless, making sure his seed stayed deep in my gut. After what seemed like a couple of minutes he pulled out. I stayed motionless, not quite sure what to expect. Before I could offer him a towel he pulled his sweatpants up to his waist. As if it was part of a well choreographed movement, he turned and walked out without saying a word. With a controlled measure the outer door quietly closed behind him. I heard his car door shut and then he started his worn out Corolla and backed out.

Private Rider

It was another boring ass night driving for Uber. This was better than a poke with a sharp stick, but sometimes it didn't feel that way. I had just picked up some drunk bitch and run her out to haughty-taughty land, also known as Sugarland. Sugarland is a suburb of Houston, TX. It's filled with McMansions, high noses, and entitled people who think they are better than everyone else. This rider was no different. After I dropped her off I headed back towards downtown. I hoped that I'd get a ride before I got downtown and that it wouldn't be in the ghetto ass neighborhoods that were dangerous after dark. As I approached one of the sketchy areas I got a ping. Aw fuck I thought as I looked at the screen on my iPad. And then I smiled. The ping, or ride request, was coming from next to a gay club called "Energizer." It was popular with the Latin boys. With any luck my rider would be hot.

My pickup point was in the parking lot next to the club. I rolled up and the parking lot looked like some sort of B-rate porno going on with a half dozen couples making out and engaging in heavy groping. One couple stopped and one of the guys waved at me. I was glad as sometimes you have to text and call people to remind them that you are there. The couple came over to the car and stopped behind my car to make out a little more. I smiled because I thought it was cute. I wasn't entirely sure if they were trying to keep me from seeing them, or if they were just really that hot for each other. They opened the door and continued making out. My rider's name was Jesus and his love of the night was saying "Oh Jesus" as they were making out. Finally he got in and I verified where we were going. I quickly realized Jesus didn't speak English and I didn't speak enough Spanish to do more than order some Tacos and a Coke. Jesus wasn't much to look at, maybe 5'8", 160#, scruffy. Oh well I thought, not really any of my business. I'm just here to give homeboy a ride and make my coin. On that note, it was a fairly long ride across town. He was headed to an area South of the Astrodome. The Astrodome is a bit of a sketchy area. I didn't know much about where I was headed, other than I hadn't been there before and that wasn't a very good indicator.

Bless his heart, Jesus was trying to make small talk with me. I did my best to answer the standard questions of "Where you are from?", "Do you do this full time?", etc. It's beyond me why people ask these questions. I'm sometimes tempted to tell them, "No, this is my backup for when my prostitution clients don't call." I think the look on their faces would be priceless. Alas, I was trying to answer his questions in what little Spanish I spoke and what little English he understood. There was nothing really remarkable about this ride, at least as Uber rides go. I turned off the freeway to head down the road he lived off of. FUCK! A damned train! Uber doesn't pay much for waiting time...and sitting at a railroad crossing wasn't my idea of fun. Just what I needed. It was just us sitting at the train crossing and the train was in no hurry to go anywhere. I don't really remember why I looked in the back seat, maybe it was a noise, or maybe it was just my habit of checking on my riders to make sure they weren't silently puking up 4 drinks and Whataburger.

I did something of a doubletake when I looked back. I think it was as much because I thought my eyes were fooling me. Slowly a big smile crept over my face. Jesus asked, "You like?" I responded, "Si!" At some point he had undone his pants and pulled out one of the biggest, nicest Latino cocks I had seen. I'm very admittedly a size queen, and my ass twitched a little on seeing that meat. It was a good 9 inches long and about the thickness of a Coke bottle with a bluntly rounded head on the end. I couldn't tell if he was cut, un-cut, or semi-cut. But he was fully erect. There wasn't much I could do with it from the front seat, so I reached back to touch it. I gently wrapped my hand around his shaft and felt the warmth of his man-hood in my hand. There is something very appealing about a new cock in your hand as a bottom. I don't know if it's opportunity or conquest, but I knew I wanted that dick in my ass. I gently stroked him a little and felt some precum drip down on to my hand. He was rock hard. Without a word he started to gently thrust into my hand. I could tell he wanted to fuck, but it wasn't going to happen in the car. I let him slowly thrust into my hand as I stroked him a little and his precum oozed out. Out of the corner of my eye I saw approaching headlights, so I stopped and retreated to the front seat. By now my hole was juicing up thinking about that big Latino cock. Jesus resumed slowly stroking his meat, seeming to get a thrill out of doing it in the car. The other car pulled up behind us and stopped. I looked down the tracks and could see the end of the train approaching. Good, I thought.

We were only a couple of miles from his drop off point, but I wanted that dick pretty badly. There wasn't a good place to pull over and ride his cock in the car, so I proceeded to his place. When we got there I finished the ride on the app as he buttoned up. He looked at me and in what was his best English said, "You finish inside?" I glanced at the clock, his bulging crotch, and said "Sure!" I pulled closer to the curb to park, put away my tablet and shut off the headlights. He got out of the car and motioned for me to follow him. I got out and followed him like a hungry puppy. Instead of heading to the front door he went to the door on the side of the garage. He put his key in and unlocked it. I wondered what the hell, but then thought I'd seen stranger things. He looked back and smiled at me and motioned to follow him. I stepped inside, but it was still dark. There wasn't anything in the garage that I could see. He grabbed my hand and then slapped my ass and pulled me over to a bench. I undid my pants at about the moment he was going to rip them off of me. Without a word he pushed me over the bench, spit in his hand and then spit on my ass. I was really wishing I had some poppers about this moment. I heard the sound of a bottle being uncapped and him taking a deep breath of them. He must have known I wanted them because he thrust them in my hand and I hit them hard as he slipped that big fat cock in my ass. I moaned a little bit at which point he reached forward and put his hand over my mouth and made a "shhh" noise in my ear. I hit the poppers again hoping it would open my hole up and he would nut relatively quickly. My hole did open up for him, but that just seemed to make him more aggressive. He slowly was pumping me, getting more aggressive with every stroke. I guess at some point he forgot that he wanted to be quiet because I realized he was pounding my ass and making a bunch of racket. I wondered who else might be at this house that he didn't want knowing he was fucking some ass.

I wasn't going to be left wondering for long. A few minutes into our trip to poundtown I heard a door open and shut. Someone else had joined us but I had no idea who or what it was. Whoever it was walked over and said something I couldn't make out in Spanish, to which Jesus replied something else I couldn't make out. While I was wondering what they were saying, I felt a hand on my head. It wandered across my face and then back to my hair. The hand ran through my hair and then grabbed the back of my head and turned me. I was being pounded from behind and now I had a fat cock being thrust down my throat. It was a thick uncut cock, probably a little shorter and it's owner was taller and chunkier then Jesus. 2 for 1 special I thought, how nice. Like some sort of pig on a spit roast I was being violated at both ends. Jesus was trying to wreck my ass while his friend was trying to wreck my mouth and throat. They were thrashing me back and forth. Jesus tempo picked up a bit and next I think I knew he was thrusting deep in me, pulsing as his manhood flooded my hole with his seed. His friend was still working my throat so all I could do was take it. His friend noticed that the pumping had stopped at the other end so he pulled out and stopped abusing my throat. Jesus pulled out and my hole just sat there gaping for a second. I wasn't quite sure what to expect. Jesus slapped my ass once and thanked me in Spanish. His friend moved around to the back. I see how this was going to work. His friend put both hands on my ass and leaned over my shoulder. He said to me, "you better hit those poppers good bitch, I'm gonna wreck that hole!" With that he put the head of his cock against my ass. By now, Jesus seed was seeping out of my ass which had been stretched open nicely. The second guy thrust in with one motion, not pausing or being gentle. Good thing I was already opened up. He bottomed out and I felt his bushy pubic hair against my ass as he paused for a second. Then he started pounding it, pinning me down so I couldn't move while he drilled my hole. Jesus had tried to wreck it, but this guy was intent on destroying it. He was thicker than Jesus, but not as long... which was a good thing. I hit the poppers good and hard, to the point where I was a bit dizzy. Meanwhile he kept drilling me hard and deep. Then suddenly he stopped and pulled out. He was still holding my ass still. Then he plunged back in, and pulled out, and plunged in. He was plunge fucking me. That was hard on my ass, but it felt amazing. This went on for a few minutes and then he went back to pounding me. The pace was different this time. Sure enough after a couple of minutes I felt the characteristic pulsing of his cock unloading in me. It went on for several seconds and I could feel him flooding me good with a huge load. His cock began to shrink and slid out of me. My hole was still twitching when he pulled me to my feet. He growled, "Get dressed and get the fuck out of here you gringo whore!" Hmm, ok I thought. I didn't say anything, I just pulled up my pants and headed for the door he was holding open. As I stepped through it he said, "Good bitch" and shut it behind me. I heard the lock engage as my eyes adjusted to the dim world outside.

Commander

I had lined up a trick from Craigslist again. His stats were 29, 6'1", 190# black, and 9.5" thick. He had responded to my ass up / face down fuck and go ad a few hours after I had posted it. Overall, nothing particularly magical compared to any other trick. This one however wanted me to be lubed, and ass up when we walked in. I was not to talk to him or look at him and the room should be dark. This always posed a challenge. I wasn't about to leave my front door unlocked and let a stranger walk in. He could think that was what was going on all he wanted, but i knew better. My usual pattern was to watch through the blinds to see what showed up. Once he parked and got out I would run to the bedroom and assume hte position. So there I sat, waiting and watching. The appointed time came and went, and I begin to think I was being stood up. Just as I had about given up a Jeep Commander rolled around the corner and drove down the street. My street has a cul-de-sac at the end and I'm pretty familiar with what my neighbors drive. This wasn't a familiar car. That didn't mean anything in particular, but it was a good sign. It had dark tinted windows, so I couldn't see who or what was driving. Sure enough, a minute later it came back up the street and rolled to a stop in front of my house. The lights went off and it parked. I could see someone fiddling with a phone inside, but still couldn't see what was about to come in. This was always a good sign, as they were usually checking their phone before coming in. Sure enough the driver door opened and a thin black guy got out. Nothing particularly scary looking so I bolted to the bedroom and jumped on the bed.

It didn't seem like I had been on the bed for 5 seconds when I heard the front door open. As we had agreed the house was completely dark and quiet. I heard the door close gently behind him and the lock engage. Good, I thought, he's following instructions. I heard the soft echo of footsteps as he approached my bedroom. My guest quickly dropped his pants and shirt on the chair near the foot of the bed. Then without a word he climbed on top of me. I think sometimes the suspense is half the fun, not knowing exactly what is going to happen. I could feel his swollen cock against my ass and it was very nice, maybe a little large. Insinctively, I hit my poppers to begin loosening my hole up for him. He wasted no time putting the head of his cock against my ass and pushing it in. Like some sort of invading force he slid all the way inside me. At about that time he also slipped his arms around underneath me and put one hand around my throat. My pulse quickened a bit as I wasn't sure what he was up to. He squeezed gently around my throat and whispered in my ear to keep quiet and let him enjoy my ass. Without another word he started pounding my ass like it had slighted him. He was a good fuck, taking time to pull almost all the way out before pushing back inside and slapping his balls on my ass. I particularly enjoyed being face down ass up as I could relax and focus on taking that cock. In his case I really needed to relax because he was pounding my hole good. It seemed like he had been fucking forever, although it probably had only been a few minutes. His pace picked up steam, almost frenetically. He was really drilling me now.... and that meant only one thing, he was close to nutting. Sure enough he slammed in one last time and his seed exploded deep in my hole as he moaned. That was always my queue to start grinding against the guys cock. I called this the finish. Right when he was most sensitive I would ride that cock some more and get a few more drops of nut out of him, like some sort of perverted prize at the end. Tops always enjoyed it, and I was always hungry for that seed. After a half minute or so he pulled out and jumped off the bed. It felt as though he was pulling a snake out of my ass as he pulled out. I lay there quietly, not looking and just listening. I could feel his load oozing out of my hole as he put on his pants and shirt, then his shoes. He muttered a gruff "thanks" before striding down the hall and out the front door.

As soon as the door closed behind him I was up to go lock it. I caught a glimpse of him striding down the sidewalk and jumping into his SUV. He started the car and bolted off the curb like he was late for something. I thought to myself as he took off, what a good fuck and I hope to see that one again.

Park Wood

Why the hell was I out driving Uber on a Tuesday night I muttered to myself. Tuesday is the slowest night of the week. Slow equals low earnings. I decided I would find somewhere to sit while I waited for another ride in the Galleria district of Houston. I found a nice CVS parking lot to park in for a few minutes. CVS has the advantage of being lit like a stage at night and pretty wide open, so it's a safe place to sit still. CVS also has the advantage of having a bathroom, which is nice when you need to piss at 11pm and discover that everything is locked up.

I pulled into the CVS parking lot and decided I would avail myself of the restroom. It's a little bit of a nuisance as that means hiding anything shiny like my iPad before I get out of the car. On my way in I opened up Grindr on my iPhone to see what was in the area. I wasn't really opposed to taking a break to ride some dick. Nothing really magical on the screen, dammit. Unlike Walgreens, CVS hides it's restrooms. I think they secretly want you to piss your pants so that Sandra at the front can yell "Wet Cleanup on the Makeup Aisle" as loudly as possible to the whole store. After what seemed like an eternity, feeling like an imposter, I figured out where the damn restroom was. As I strode towards it I heard the unmistakable noise that Grindr makes when you get a message. I hoped it wasn't another fucking chatbot as I walked into the restroom. On the bright side, CVS restrooms are clean and mostly functional. Walgreens restrooms often look like someone has been in them with a baseball bat and diahrrea. I'm not really sure which problem happened first sometimes. The urinal had a bag over it, so I opted for the toilet stall. I glanced over at the divider while I was pissing and mused at the graffiti. I think it's a univeral American thing to scribble obscenities and offers on the toilet walls. "Latin for big black dick 713-555-1212" read one ad. "Call me for a magic pussy" read another. "cum-n-go gloryhole" read another with an email address. I shook my head and chuckled, and wrapped up my business. I pulled out my phone to see what Grindr had for me, half expecting to see some bullshit "sex-party" scambot. I opened up the messages, hoping it wasn't another fucking tap. Whoever invented those taps should have their dick painted with glitter and be left tied up in a room with 25 hyper active kittens on catnip I thought to myself. My iPhone was getting a little long in the tooth and speed was no longer a feature to be found on it with Grindr. You'd think that a list of faggots hunting dick and ass shouldn't take that much power to display, but alas it seemed to require winding the phone up. Finally, I got the messages open. It wasn't a damn tap, but an actual message. The profile photo looked just like what Kitty wanted. A headless black torso that was pretty ripped. I opened up the message to see what it was. "I want to fuck you, outside. Now!" read the first message. The second message was a beautiful black cock, it looked pretty damn big, maybe 9 and above average girth, but nothing to call Guiness about. I sent back "When / Where?" and a picture of my ass. I put my phone back in my pocket as I debated if this was flake-o-matic or the deal was going to close and kitty was gonna get some nut. I walked out of the store without buying anything, feeling a tad guilty. I reassured myself that I was saving 2 or 3 trees by not buying something and being stuck with a 15 to 20 foot long receipt for a bottle of soda and a candy bar.

I got back in the car and checked my Grindr messages again. "Now, Outside... come get me" followed by a location. It was pretty close by, so I texted back, "Sure" with details of what I was driving. Before I headed that way I looked at Google Maps to see if I could figure out where we'd fuck. The last thing I needed was to get caught/busted taking dick in my ass. I drove down Westheimer Road, a major street in Houston and turned left into Galleria Ghetto Apartment Sprawl. There must have been 1500 units in this place. Thank God I wasn't doing an Uber pickup here I thought. It's always a pain in the ass to find someone in a place like this. I texted fuck boy to see what was up and he messaged me back as to where he was.

I pulled up and fuck boy hopped in. I introduced myself as Will, and he said his name was Dante. I drove out of the apartment complex and headed West and South towards where I thought there would be somewhere to fuck. While I was driving he pulled his shorts down and whipped out a nice thick black cock. I put my hand back there and felt him and was quite impressed. That was going to be some great dick when I found a place. We tried a couple of streets and I didn't see anything that I felt like I could defent do a police officer if we got caught. Just as I was getting frustrated trying to find a place I spotted a park on the map. Just as well, I needed to piss again. It was a midsize City park complete with basketball courts, tennis courts, and a dark wooded area. I pulled around to the side and parked by the port-a-can that passed as a bathroom here. Dante Fuckboy followed me into the handicap port-a-can and we debated fucking there. I told him we would be better outside where we wouldn't have to explain two of us in the shitter.

We exited the port-a-can and headed towards the back of the park. It was mostly dark and quiet, just like I like an outdoor fuck scene. We walked a few hundred yards to what I figured was the most remote, darkest spot of the fence / tree line. I had no idea what was on the other side of the fence, but it was closed whatever it was, and it was also dark. I asked Dante if he though this would work and he whipped his cock out, rock hard. I guess that was my answer and so I dropped down to suck him. After a minute or so he

said, "Okay, dats enough, gimme dat ass white boy." As instructed I lubed up my ass and got on all four's by a tree. He wasted no
time in putting the head of his cock against my hole and beginning
to work it in. I hit my poppers almost as much as a self-defense
mechanism as anything else. Like magic, my hole opened up and he
slipped in balls deep. He paused for a second before saying, "Boy
you got good pussy." "Yes Sir!" I replied. He started to pump me
while holding himself with one hand on the tree and one hand on my
shoulder for leverage. He slipped in and out pounding me quietly
with a purpose while I watched for anyone who might notice a white
boy getting used by a black guy at night in a park. It seemed like
he was taking forever when he finally picked up the pace and stayed
in me. Suddenly, like most guys, he slammed it in, moaned a little
and I could feel his cock pulse as he injected his seed marking my
ass as having been used by him. I was pinned down at a disadvan-
tage and couldn't do much other than just take it. I normally like
to grind back a bit, but that wasn't happening. He deftly slid out
of me and pushed himself up at the same time. I quietly stood up
and pulled my pants up, and glanced at him. He smiled back at me
and said, "You have good pussy, I want it again tomorrow." "Okay I
answered." We walked back to the car as I thought how in the hell
would we explain this if a cop drove up. I had vaseline and poppers
in my pocket and cum dripping out of my ass. My ass felt squishy
which is one of my favorite feelings. We made it back to the car
without incident, hopped in and left.

I drove back to his place mostly reflecting on the good sex
and occassionally answering a question. When we got there he
directed me where to drop him off. Before he got out he leaned
forward to give me a good long kiss at about the same time some
dumbass pulled up behind us, mad that I was blocking the gate. No
big deal, I said bye to Dante Fuckboy and waved to the fool behind
me. I had my Uber light on and just played stupid like I was dropping a passenger off.

Big Bend

Josh and I had decided to go to Big Bend National Park almost on a whim. It was New Years and the desert is surprisingly mild and surprisingly busy at this time of year. Big Bend National Park is a really long way from Houston where we lived. It's a 12 hour drive, all without leaving Texas. When we entered the park, we paid our fee to the nice lady at the gate and proceeded in. Our plan was to back country camp in a tent each night and to visit several parts of the park. We had driven my Jeep Wrangler which was well suited to the park's dirt roads. The only downside was having a soft top like most Jeeps at the time. Our first night was getting near so we drove to the East side of the park and down a dirt road / trail. After enough bumps and mild hills we found a nice spot to camp and proceeded to setup camp as it was getting dark. Both of us were entirely too tired to be horny, so we ate dinner and went to bed. Having driven all day we were glad to be sleeping in a tent, on rocks in the desert surrounded by plants with spines and god knows what slithery or crawly critters.

On day 2 we decided to explore the lower river road that ran alongside the Rio Grande River. We broke camp and headed down the road towards the RV campground. I guess someone in an RV would think it was fabulous, but it looked more like a parking lot with some grass dividers, a few trees, and a restroom that only satan could love. We stopped in to use the restroom and discovered that it had coin operated showers. The most disgusting coin operated showers in the universe. There was about an inch of stagnant water on the floor, saloon style shower doors and a layer of slime that looked as though the Spanish Conquistadors might have installed it. Josh reminded me we were camping, and this wasn't the Hilton. I shot him a nasty look and told him it was the Hellton. Wiht that we departed the Happy Ranch or whatever goofy name the National Park Service called that campground We headed to the road that ran along the river. It was marked 4x4 only on the map and I was a little excited. Gravel wasn't exactly a challenge for my Jeep. The challenge was not getting behind another car and breathing the voluminous dust that the gravel roads generated. We had fun exploring the ruins of something called the Mariscal Mine. According to the signs they had mined Mercury here. I was surprised it wasn't a EPA superfund site. Afterwards we headed down by the river for lunch. I guess at some point it was Grande, but it really wasn't anything special to see. When you could see it. The banks were overgrown with brush. We were exploring the road and turned towards the river down a side road. After about 500 yards we came to a clearing that seemed to double as a parking area. We were completely surrounded by brush about 10 feet high and couldn't see anyone or anything. We decided this was a good enough spot to enjoy lunch and explore a little on foot. Lunch was sandwiches and chips. Tasty and easy. Exploring on foot didn't get far. It turned out that the little area we were on was surrounded by a 12 foot gravel drop off. As we got back to the Jeep Josh stopped and turned towards me and leaned back on the bumper. It was a beautiful sunny day and the weather was just right to enjoy. As I walked towards him, Josh said, "Hey faggot, suck my cock." I stopped and looked around, surprised he had said that. He knew I hated being called a Faggot. I shot him a smirk and a short, "no!" I was his boyfriend, not his bitch.... or so I thought. By this time I was about arm's length from him and he repeated his demand, "Suck my cock you faggot!" By this time I could see he was getting turned on. There was a nice bulge in his pants. I debated what I should say back. I didn't really want to play in the open in broad daylight. I guess it was obvious that I was debating how to react. He reached out and put one hand on my shoulder and the other behind my head. He pushed me down and pulled me towards his crotch. Before I could say anything he said to me, "You are going to suck me off faggot!" He pulled my face into his crotch and he was fully erect at this point. He had a nice 8 inch cock, avg thickness, but it curved slightly down and was very easy to deepthroat. He pushed his cock against my face through his shorts. I could tell he wanted to get off. "Pull it out," he commanded. I obliged....looking around to make sure we were alone. "Suck it bitch!," he ordered. This was kind of hot, he wasn't usually demanding. I put my tongue on his meat and slowly started to work him. He was turned on and oozing a bit of precum which tasted sweet. I slowly wet the head of his cock and then the shaft. Working him deeper with each pass up and down his cock. Each veign on his cock was standing up and he was rock hard. His hand was on the back of my head and started to push me down. He liked being balls deep in whatever he was using to get off. Be that my throat or my ass. That was part of what I liked about him. Once I got him turned on he turned into a beast. At the moment I was pretty sure I was sucking the cock of a beast. He was gradually getting more active, pumping my throat and holding the back of my head with both hands. Occassionally he would gag me. By this time I was hard as well and had my cock out, stroking it as he fucked my mouth and throat. I was a little worried that we might get caught, but at this point I just wanted to get off. I knew in the back of my mind that once he started to fuck my mouth, he was going to use my ass next. I wasn't sure I was clean enough back there, but then again that had never stopped him before. We had wipes as a backup in case shitty kitty made an unwelcome appearance. Josh was fully into my throat now and had stopped leaning on the bumper of my Jeep. He had both of his hands on the back of my neck and was letting me breathe when his cock wasn't down my throat. His precum tasted fantastic, as always. He paused for a second and growled at me to turn around on my knees. He placed me between the Jeep and his body, pushing me back against the bumper with the head of his cock in my mouth. Next, he put both hands on the bumper and used it as a hand hold as he started to pump my throat again. This time there was no backing off or getting away, he was slowly working up in tempo. I had a pretty good idea what was going to come next, but I was enjoying the hell out of him using my mouth. I was still worried about getting caught or having someone drive up on us. But the chances were pretty remote because we would hear anyone in a vehicle long before they arrived.

Josh was pretty worked up by now. I knew he was going to fuck me. Anytime he had ever fucked my throat that was just an appetizer for him using my ass. He had been pumping my throat with me pinned against the Jeep bumper for a few minutes now. I was really wishing for some poppers, because it would make getting drilled a little easier. Up until now I had thought this was a pretty spontaneous fuck session. What happened next convinced me that Josh had been planning to use me all morning. He stopped fucking my throat and pulled his beautiful cock out of my mouth. It just hung there, glistening from my spit and his precum, about an inch or two in front of my face. I could still smell his man scent all over my face. With my tongue I expertly flicked a hair out from between my teeth. I glanced up to see what was going on and he was just watching me and smiling. He reached down and lifted me up with his hands under my arms. I wasn't that much smaller than him, but he was well built and well hung. Always a nice combination for a hungry bottom. He pulled me up and gave me a good deep kiss and then growled at me, "Assume the position boy!" With that command he spun me around and pushed me over the hood of the Jeep. He reached down into his pants and pulled out a packet of lube and some poppers. He took a hit on the poppers and thrust them forward to me and said, "Take these!" I knew right then that he had been prepared to fuck me, and that meant he had quietly wanted it all day. He lubed up his manhood and then slipped into my ass. This was hot, he was fucking me in broad daylight, 200 feet from the Mexican border in a beautiful National Park. Slowly at first, he opened my hole up. Too slowly I thought. I knew he was pretty turned on based on how he had been using my throat. I figured maybe he was just edging a bit, or maybe loosening me up good. Sure enough, after a few minutes of slow, deep thrusts he grabbed a hold of the bumper he had me bent over and started pounding me hard enough to rock the Jeep back and forth. I was enjoying the hell out of it. I absolutely loved being pounded and he knew it. I also knew he got off on fucking hard and knowing I liked it. I was moaning and hitting my poppers periodically. We'd been together long enough that I knew his increasing tempo meant he was about to flood my hole. He started making alot more noise and drilling me hard and then suddenly thrust in and flooded me. I could feel

80

him pulsing in synch with his moans and knew his seed was flooding deep inside me. I think at about that point it clicked with him that we were having some pretty risky sex. He usually would stay in me for a few minutes. This time he pulled out and pulled his pants up. That was my queue to do the same. I stood up and turned around and he put his arms around me. We kissed for a few minutes and I thanked him for some hot sex. We both got back in the Jeep with a big smile.

Latin Fusion

I was working from home, or rather working-it from home. Another dreary day of death by meeting and email torture. The guy I worked for was a complete ass. One of those Scotch-on-the-rocks types that thought he knew everything. He treated people as expendable and had been blowing my email all morning. He wanted to fire one of the people on my team and I was trying to keep him busy long enough for this to blow over. In the meanwhile I had my whore-mail up on my second monitor. Whore-mail was what I called my dedicated gmail account for craigslist hookups. it was about 11:30am and one of my Latino regulars hit me up. He was nothing particularly spectacular. I think he did sales of some sort, so he was clean cut. He wasn't particularly well hung, but he was very piggy and always a fun fuck. Probably 7 and average. He wanted to know if I had time for a lunch fuck. Of course, I replied. I had cleaned out when I showered this morning and was in need of a distraction from the bullshit of work. I wasn't really expecting the next email. His next email asked if a friend could join. I generally had a dim view of 3 ways as normally someone was 3rd wheel. I hesitated, and then I asked what he had in mind. He assured me that both of them are tops. Fuck it I thought. Sure, I replied.

At the appointed time I watched his little Acura sedan pull up. One thing I could always appreciate is that he was punctual. That was so much nicer than people who would tell you they'll be there in 30 minutes, but not specify which 30 minutes they meant. I wondered where his buddy was. I wouldn't wonder very long, an average looking blue Ford Focus pulled up behind him as he got out. Apparently this was his friend. Not much to look at I thought as I watched through the blinds. While Joe was clean-cut, his friend was scruffy / raggedy. Longish hair, pulled back in one of those stupid man-bun things. Half-shaven. Not particularly tall. I hoped he was well hung. They both approached the house, so I went to the door. As I always did for my lunch hook-ups, I was naked and stood behind the door as I answered it.

I greeted both of them and Joe introduced his friend as Raul as I shut the door behind them. I told them it was nice to see them as I walked to the bedroom. I pointed to the folding chair and told them one of them could put their clothes on there. I looked around trying to decide where I could suggest for the other one to put his clothes. I pulled a folding wooden TV-stand away from the side of the bed and said that would work for the other one's clothes. It was clean-ish and was serving as a night stand. In theory, one day I would build/buy furniture, but for now temporary living would work. While they got undressed I turned down the AC and closed the blinds in the bedroom. I prefered a dim/dark scene for fucking. It just was more fun.

I got down on my knees and started sucking Joe hard. I was curious to see what Raul had to offer. My curiosity wouldn't survive long. What he lacked in appearance he made up for in cock. That was always nice with hookups. The reality is that with hookups appearance wasn't as important as performance. A pretty boy with a small dick wasn't as much fun as an ugly boy with a big dick. Raul was alot closer to the second. I guess Joe noticed me starting at Raul's cock while I was sucking his. He stepped back and motioned for Raul to step over. By now Joe was fully erect. He was probably 7 and average thickness, maybe slightly skinnier than average. It was a nice cock and he was a fun fuck. Raul wasted no time in getting hard and slipping in my willing mouth. He was precumming a little bit and had a nice patch of fur on his chest. I thought to myself he would probably clean up nicely, but whatever, I was just after the dick. After a few more minutes I stopped and suggested we get on the bed. Lunch fucks move at a different tempo and it's important to get down to business.

We all three got on the bed. Raul laid back on the pillows and was slowly stroking his cock. I took this as an invite to straddle him and ride that cock. I'd handle Joe in a minute I thought. I started to ride Raul and he pulled me down to make out with him. This was turning out to be pretty hot, but it was about to get alot hotter. As I was riding and Raul was pumping Joe asked if I'd ever been double fucked. I chuckled and said no. He replied that we could fix that and I thought for a second and said "bring it on." Both of these guys were about the right size for me to do that. Joe moved in behind me and pushed his cock up against my hole and Raul's cock which was already in. My ass must have been particularly hungry that day as his cock just slipped in. It was hot feelin these two guys in me at once. Each of them rock hard and pre-cumming a bit. I wasn't sure how the mechanics of this were going to work, but not for me to wonder. Joe started pumping from behind and Raul started to gently pump from under me. It felt fantastic and I wondered how long these two were going to last. Joe was tweaking my nipples from behind and Raul was watching intently as I moaned and rolled my eyes. Raul was getting close and said so. He started to moan quite a bit and I could feel his hot seed pulsing into my hole. This set Joe off who immediately shot a huge load. It was really hot to feel both of them pulsing and jizzing in me at once. Joe no sooner finished nutting and he slipped out and backed off. I didn't say anything, but was glad. I eased off of Raul and thanked both of them for a hot fuck. Raul jumped up and started to get dressed right away. Saying he had somewhere to be he excused himself and darted out the door. By this time Joe had gotten dressed. He usually took off after he got off and this was no exception. I thanked him for a good lunch and shut the door behind him.

Railrod

       Growing up I had always had a fascination with trains. As a young gay man that fascination had never really gone away and instead had grown to include the hot men who ran the trains. I think there was an element of excitement to the deep rumbling, raw power that a train possesses. In my mind this extended to the men who ran them. I often enjoyed walking in the park to clear my mind, get some exercise and to think. Houston, where I lived at the time, had wonderful Memorial Park. One side of the park is "wild" and less used then the other, which is manicured with a golf course and tennis courts. The edge of the wild side has train tracks that run through it and there are frequently trains sitting there waiting for clearance. The trail is a rarely used dirt road that I think the electric company uses to check the power lines that run through a grassy area between the park and the train tracks. If one follows the trail you eventually come to Buffalo Bayou, a stream of sorts that is intertwined with Houston physically and historically. This particular part of the bayou where it intersects with the train bridge is unlike any part of Houston you would recognize. It has steep sandy banks, some rocks in the stream bed and the gurgle of water running through it. It reminds me of places that are not Houston, and thus it's a favorite place to go and sit or walk. It's sometimes fun to go up on the bridge and throw gravel from the tracks into the water.

       It was a nice Spring day, on a Thursday. I was walking along the trail to get to the back half where people weren't as common. This was my usual routine and it was around 5:30pm, a little before sunset, but an otherwise nice day. The only downside to the approaching evening was the awful mosquitos that would soon be out. Fortunately the bug spray was still working and would keep them away for a while unless they could find a vulnerable spot. As I walked I began to hear the low rumble of an approaching train, so I hurried my pace to a spot where I could watch. Normaly the trains were Northbound through here, but this one sounded like it was coming from the North. Almost on queue the sound grew louder as I got closer to my spot where I could see down the tracks in both directions. This spot would put me about 20 feet from the tracks and give me a great view. Close enough to feel the train without being in a dangerous spot. He wasn't going very fast which I thought was odd. Usually the trains came through here doing 35 or 40 mph which seemed much faster than it really must have been. That or they were already sitting here, facing North when I saw them. He was crawling up the tracks maybe doing 5 miles per hour. I'd never seen one come through this slowly and was intrigued to see what was going on. As he drew closer I realized he was coming to a stop and from the looks of it he was going to stop somewhere near me. Slowlly the engines lumbered closer, now going slower than ever. I could have walked and kept up with them by the time they got near me. At this point I had retreated to between the bushes lest I get in trouble for being this close to the train. I watched as the two engines in the lead pulled abreast of me and then past me before coming to a stop just before the bridge, 200 feet to my left. The engines were so close I could feel the ground shaking as they crawed past. When they train had stopped the engineer must have hit the parking brake. The train made a loud noise like air escaping and all the cars seemed to lock up. I could barely see that the brake had been set by looking at the wheels. It was getting dark by now. I was curious what was going on so I stayed still and just watched.

I wouldn't have to wait long, the side door of the cab opened and an older white guy climbed down. He was talking to someone but I couldn't make out who or what he was saying. As climbed down a younger black guy poked his head out and they continued talking. The older white guy walked out to the trail and proceeded toward the parking lot. I watched him pass where I was standing in between the bushes and trees. He didn't notice me and I wasn't moving anyway. I'd never seen anyone get off the train here, much less go anywhere. I looked back towards the parking lot and realized a car had appeared at the trail head. I guess he was being picked up. An interesting crew change for sure. I watched the few minutes as he got to the car, got in and it left. Strangely, nobody had gotten out.

It was dark now and so I decided to walk down the trail towards where the train engine had stopped. As I got to about even with the train cab a trinity of stupid things happened. I looked over and realized the black guy was taking a piss off the train, at about the same time I tripped and he noticed me. There was just enough moonlight for me to see him and him to see me. I couldn't tell for sure, but it looked like he had a really nice dick. Most of the time a guy would put his cock away when another guy saw it. He was staring right at me and kept it out, as if he was daring me to watch him piss off his train. When he finished pissing he kept looking at me and shook his cock a little. I think he realized I was looking at it. He kept gently shaking it and I could tell he was getting hard. I was standing still, just watching. After a minute or so he was fully hard, a good 9 inches or so, and fat. It was a pretty dick, and the guy it was on wasn't bad either, at 6' 220# with his hair shaved bald. I could tell he worked out because he was built. I was about 30 feet away and staring at his cock. He said nothing but was staring directly at me. He turned and climbed down the ladder and stood next to the train. He was now a little closer to me and still hard as a rock. Finally he said hello to me and told me to quit staring and come suck it like a good faggot. I glanced around nervously and then did as I was told.

86

It was bigger than it looked and I gasped a little as I dropped to my knees. He was dripping a little precum as I took him genty in my mouth. I could tell he was the type to dominate and he wasted no time in proving me correct. He put his hand on the back of my head and began to force himself down my throat. Gently at first, but I could feel the power in his hand. He was working my throat over and I was enjoying gagging on his meat. I noticed that his thrusts were getting more forceful and wondered if he was going to nut. He was moaning a little, but not much. I didn't think he was ready, but sometimes I'd been surprised by guys like this. He didn't seem to be concerned about getting caught which seemed odd. I was worried his coworker was going to come back or someone would walk up on us. He paused and pulled his cock out of my mouth. He asked me, "your ass clean faggot?" "Yes sir," I replied. I felt his other hand on my head and he grabbed me and pulled me up. Once I was on my feet he pushed me towards the train. He said to me, "You're going to get fucked. You can either lean against the engine or I'm going to put you on the ground and take your hole."

I thought to myself, "Gee I have a choice," as I leaned against the engine. Luckily I was near the ladder going up and I grabbed a hold of it. I could feel the heat from him standing be-hind me. He coughed up some some spit and spit in his hand. I guess that's how I'm going to get fucked I thought. Sure enough he squatted down and spit in my ass and then stood back up and put the head of his cock against my hole. I was about to find out if he was a beast or just beast-like. A beast would just shove it in. For-tunately for me he was just beast-like. I heard the distinctive sound of sniffing poppers behind me. "Here!" he commanded as he thrust the bottle over my shoulder. "Don't spill them, faggot!" he finished. I didn't need to be told twice or invited. I took a good long hit on the poppers as he started to slide in me, stretching me open. After a minute he stopped and squatted down again and spat in my hole. He then stood up and smacked my ass and put the tip of his meat against my hole again. This time he slid half way in and told me, "you better loosen up, I don't have all night and you're going to earn this nut faggot boy." "Yes sir," I replied. He pulled it out a bit and then slid deeper. I was moaning and he put a hand over my mouth and slid all the way in. I wanted to scream, but I knew not to. I squirmed a bit and he just held me still and let my ass adjust to his cock. He was throbbing inside me. About as I caught my breath he began to pump my hole. Slowly at first and then picking up pace pretty quickly til he was pounding me. The poppers were wearing off but he was pounding me too hard to take a hit again. I just held on with one hand and held the poppers in the other. He was like a machine, a beast machine, just pounding away at my hole. As I was wondering how long he would go he sped up and groaned a little and then thrust deep in me and stopped. He moaned a little and said he was dumping. I felt his cock pulse as he shot deep in my hole, filling it with his creamy man-seed. He held it in for a few seconds and then pulled out.

I didn't say anything. He was buttoning his pants up and I took that as the queue to pull mine up. I handed him his poppers back and pulled my pants up. Before I could say anything he said, "Get out of here faggot!" I replied, "Thank you sir!" quietly. He said, "You're welcome. Now get out of here." With that he climbed back in the engine and I walked off towards the parking lot. As I walked back towards the parking lot I wondered if that was a regular occurrence that I had somehow been oblivious too in the past. I wondered how I could have missed that sort of action in the past. I heard an approaching vehicle as I reached the edge of the parking lot. I looked up to see a Union Pacific Truck coming around the corner. It was a 4 door model, Chevy with a open bed. It parked and two middle aged white guys got out. I said "Hello" as I walked by and they said "Good evening" back. Oh how good of an evening I thought.

I got back in my RX7 and sat there for a moment. I could feel his load seeping out of my wrecked hole. I watched to see what was going on. The truck wasted no time in driving off and the two white guys set off down the trail towards the train. After about 10 minutes I heard the woosh of air filling the brakes. I heard the engines spool up and the train slowly chugged away, taking Mr. Fuckbeast with it.

Dining Out

The clerk, Tyrone, had just started his shift at the seedy bookstore. It was another unremarkable day in a dismal building that reeked of urine, poppers, and trash. The building was a low slung convenience store that in better days had been probably been a 7-11 store. Not a nice one that offered gas, but a dumpy one that was crammed on a corner in the inner city of Houston. Now it was an adult bookstore. Not the nice one where you go to get your rocks off, but a seedy, nasty one where the desparate, the determined, and the depraved go to hold court. On any given day you could find drag hookers, addicts, and desparate businessmen in the back trading pleasures. The front area was presentable enough with it's menagerie of lube, dildos, and sexcessories. There were the requisite blow up dolls as well. There was also a beat up brown wooden door with one of those diamond shaped windows in the middle. It might as well have been the door to hell as far as Tyrone was concerned. He tried to never go back there. Behind that door were collection of 12 "viewing rooms." Each was appointed with a crab infested cushion, a couple of buttons, a crappy speaker, and cum-stained walls. Half the doors didn't lock worth a shit. Some rooms had bonus appointments like used needles, the occassional condom, and sticky or stinky toilet paper.

Tyrone had just started to price a new case of poppers to put on the shelf. These things sold pretty well and even folks from the gayborhood would stop in to get their fix. About 4 bottles in to the case of 72 the front door swung open. Tyrone looked up just in time to see one of the regulars, who we will just call Cumtesia stride through the door with a scruffy looking Latino man behind him. Tyrone smiled and called out "Hey Girl!" Cumtesia was about 6'4" and 170 pounds. Tall, slender, and reportedly all donkey where it mattered. His Latino trade was about 5'4" and looked like he had just walked off a construction site. Very typical for the clientele at this store. Cumtesia seemed to be in a mood. Normally he was pretty chatty, but not tonight. He looked at Tyrone, then looked at his Trade and muttered, "Two for first class." Tyrone replied, "That will be $12." Cumtesia looked at the little Latin man and said, "Jose, I told you this shit ain't free.... pay the man." Jose dug in his pocket and pulled out a $20. He handed it to Tyrone while saying to Cumtesia, "Yes Dear." Before Tyrone could make change, Jose asked him, "How much for dee Jungle Juice?" "Platinum, Premium, or Regular?" Tyrone asked back. "Pleetinum," Jose replied. "$25," Tyrone said. Jose looked a little surprised, but dug out another $20 and put it on the counter. It was moist from something. Tyrone handed over the poppers and put the money in the till. "Enjoy your visit," he told the couple. Cumtesia took what seemed like 3 steps and vanished through the door to the viewing area. Jose straggled along behind like a lost puppy. Tyrone was sure Cumtesia was gonna work that boy over. He hoped it wouldn't get messy, but then it wasn't his problem to clean it up thankfully. He just had to sit through the racket they'd be making back there for an hour and a half.

Tyrone returned to pricing his case of poppers. This was the life of a bookstore clerk. Utter boredome punctuated by brief episodes of insanity, terror, or stupidity. He'd been held up twice and had more arguments than he could shake a stick at. About twice a night someone would proposition him and ask if he had a big black cock. It turned his stomach to think of fucking the customers who came in here. Most of them were absolute trash!

About 10 bottles forward he heard a scream coming from the back. It sounded vaguely Latino, but one could never no. Sensing that an episode of instanity, terror, or stupidity was about to start he stopped what he was working on. Sure enough about 15 seconds later the ratty brown door exploded open to reveal a new contestant. Someone he had never seen before, a short, pudgy white guy stood there. He looked like a miniature Danny DeVito, all of maybe 5'3" hairier than a wild pig, and half bald. He was dressed, sort of, in garters, a pink fishnet top, and some sort of skirt thing that looked like it had come from the Hobby Lobby DIY table. The skirt thing was bright orange, maybe it had been half off from Halloween last month Tyrone thought. Before he could ask what was going on, the new contestant moaned in pain and said, "Help, you have to help me!" "Okay, what's up doc?" Tyrone replied. "It's stuck! Fuck it hurts!" said the dwarf crossdresser. "What's stuck? What is your name?" Tyrone replied. "Ryan. Don't tell anyone." Ryan replied. "My wife has no idea." He added. "What's stuck?" Asked Tyrone. "My Toy. Can you pull it out?" Ryan said. "Your Toy?" Tyrone asked. What the fuck he thought. I don't get paid enough to pull shit out of people's asses. He knew instinctively that this involved something up this guy's ass. "Yes, my toy slipped in and I can't get it out. It hurts like fuck. You have to help me!" Ryan replied. Tyrone looked him up and down and instead of replying reached for the phone. It was a Lemon Yellow $12.99 Radio Shack special. It was touch tone and had been dropped so many times that it was a wonder it worked. With his thumb on the hook, Tyrone asked, "What kind of toy is it?" Ryan replied, "It's a plantain. Please you gotta pull it out for me." Tyrone wanted to laugh, but it wouldn't help. He took his thumb off the hook and dialed 911.

"911 what is your emergency?" the operator asked. Tyrone replied, "I need an ambulance to 1506 Westheimer, Dine In News." "One moment please." The operator replied. "I'm transferring your call. Please stay on the line." "I understand you need an ambulance to 1506 Westheimer, Dine In News." came the man's voice. "Yes," replied Tyrone. "Okay we have one headed your way, what is the nature of the emergency." asked the dispatcher. By now, Ryan had a look of absolute horror on his face. Tyrone looked Ryan up and down and replied into the phone, "Look, don't hang up on me, I work here. I'm not making up what I'm about to tell you. I have a customer who says he has something stuck in his ass and he needs help. I promise I'm not a prank call." After a long pause, the dispatcher replied, "Look this is a recorded line for real emergencies." Tyrone cut him off, "I'm not making this up I need an ambulance here to help this customer." As if on cue Ryan started screaming that he was in pain. Before the dispatcher could say anything else, Tyrone added, "1506 Westheimer, Dine In News, seedy building on the corner of Jackson and Westheimer." And with that he hung up. He looked at Ryan and growled, "You better not be making this shit up. I think they are coming. I'm not pulling anything out of your ass. Six bucks gets you in back and that's it!" Ryan was nearly in tears at this point. It was obviosu that he was in pain.

After what seemed like an eternity Tyrone could hear a siren in the distance getting closer. He hoped it was the ambulance. Ryan was going on about how he didn't mean for this to happen, the plantain had just slipped. Tyrone told him, "It's going to be fine. I think that's your hero I hear now." This seemed to calm Ryan down a bit. Sure enough the siren was much louder now and the ambulance pulled into the parking lot. Never a dull moment Tyrone thought. All for $12/hr. Two paramedics walked in through the front door. One was a nice blond man, about 28, 6'2" 210, well worked out, buzz cut. The other was a short black woman, 5'8" 175. She had a no-nonsense air about her. She was carrying what looked like an oversize tackle box. Before either could ask, Tyrone pointed to Ryan and said, "Thanks for coming, he needs your help." The blond took the lead and asked Ryan, "I'm Vince, what's going on?" Ryan replied, "I got a toy stuck, I'm sorry, I didn't mean to." Vince looked at the black woman, and then before he could say anything, she said, "What do you mean you got it stuck? What is it and where is it stuck?" Ryan replied, "In my ass, a plantain." Her nametag said Tawanda, and she broke what seemed like an eternity of silence, "So you have a bananna in your ass?" Ryan replied back sheepishly, "Yes it hurts like hell, can you pull it out?" At this point both medics looked at Tyrone, who replied, "I just work here." Tawanda looked at Vince and said, "This one is yours. I ain't pullin no banana out of nobody's ass!" She added, "I don't get paid for that shit. Sorry. Not Sorry." Vince looked at Ryan and said, "Okay so you really have a banana in your ass?" Ryan said, "Yes it's a plantain. It has a rubber on if that helps." Tawanda looked at Tyrone and wanted to just bust out laughing, but that would have been highly inappropriate. She'd already been written up last month for telling someone to "Shut the fuck up and sit your ass down." Her girl-friend wasn't putting out and she was pretty frustrated. It was coming to work with her. Vince thought for a second and replied, "Okay well you have two options, I can pull it out here, or we can take you to the hospital. What do you want?" "Here?" Ryan replied. "Yes Here," Vince replied. Tyrone piped up, "Hey try not to make a mess." Tawanda shot him a dirty look and said, "Really? You called us to get a banana from someone's ass and you don't want us to make a mess?" Tyrone shot back, "Not my banana, not my ass, don't make it my mess!"

Ryan spoke up, "Fine whatever, it hurts like hell, just get it out." As if on queue, Tawanda set down the box and got out some KY. Vince had gloves on and told Ryan, "Bend over and relax. This isn't going to hurt me a bit, but it might be a little uncom-fortable for you. I have to reach in with my fingers and try to grab it." Ryan replied, "I'm not really into fisting, but okay." "Just pretend it's a giant banana then," replied Vince. Tyrone laughed a little and Tawanda shot him a dirty look. He knew it was not right, but it was just too funny. As if on queue, thump thump thump thump was com-ing from the back. Cumtesia must be nailing Jose Tyrone thought. Vince was working his fingers and hand into Ryan's ass and Tawanda looked like she wanted to ask what the noise was, but didn't want to know. Ryan was yelling loudly that it hurt and Vince was telling him he almost had it. This was a certified shit show thought Tyrone. About that time the front door opened and a officer from Houston Police Department walked in. Fuck, thought Tyrone. The officer looked at the medics and his eyes got wide as he saw one had his hand up Ryan's ass. He then looked at Tyrone and Tawanda, and said, "I saw the ambulance and just stopped to make sure everything is okay. It looks like you have the situation in hand. I'm going to go now." And with that he backed out of the door and left. Vince said loudly, "It's coming, don't move!" Ryan yelled some more, and Vince held up the offending Plantain. Sure enough the damn thing had a condom on it. Tawanda looked like she was gonna hurl. Vince had a wicked smile on his face. Ryan said "Thank you so much."

About 5 seconds later the door to the back burst open and Jose stepped in. He looked a little worse for the wear. He looked at the plantain which was still in the air in Vince's hand, Ryan's outfit, and Tyrone. He then bolted for the door while saying loudly,

"Jesus Protegeme" (Jesus Protect Me). Tawanda looked at Tyrone and then said to Vince, "You got your prize, let's get out of here." Ryan looked at both of them and said, "Thanks guys", pulled up his stocking and strode through the door to the back. Vince looked at Tyrone and asked, "Trash can?" "Yea sure, right here. Thank you again," replied Tyrone. "All in a day's work," replied Vince. By this time Tawanda had closed up her go box and was back out at the truck. "I get it," replied Tyrone.

Vince looked at Tyrone and then said, "Hey, I have seen you at Heaven a few times. Take down my number and call me sometime. 713-524-7369." "For Real," asked Tyrone. "Yea, if you want." replied Vince. "Okay, I'm off on Wednesday and Thursdays," replied Tyrone. Vince replied, "Great. Look forward to hearing from you sexy. I gotta go, the battle axe is waiting for me outside." Tyrone laughed and said, "Okay stud."

It seemed like the door had barely shut behind Vince when an imposing blond woman walked in. Tyrone didn't know who she was, but he did know she wasn't the typical customer. She looked around in disgust and walked straight to the counter. She looked at Tyrone and said, "Hey boy, I'm looking for my shithead husband, have you seen him?" She held out her phone with a picture of Ryan on it. Before Tyrone could answer, she added, "That son of a bitch is in here somewhere. I have tracking on his phone. His sick ass might be wearing women's clothes." This woman was an absolute bitch. Tyrone thought for a second and then said, "Nope, haven't seen him." "Well can I look around? What's through that door?" she asked. "That's the men only area," Tyrone replied. "Well I want to go back there," replied the woman. "No, you can't go back there," replied Tyrone. Before she could reply Cumtesia strode through the door. She looked at him in disgust and before she could say anything he said in a deep gravelly voice, "What the fuck you looking at bitch?" "I don't quite know, what am I lookin at?" the woman replied. "The best dick in Montrose, but I ain't got time for no worn out middle age racist pussy today," Cumtesia shot back. Before angry woman could reply, "And you better check your shit before someone packs your ass out the door." Cumtesia strode out the door leaving angry woman and Tyrone. Angry woman, demanded again to go in the back. Tyrone replied, "Look it ain't happening. You need to go or I'm calling the police." "Fine boy, I'll leave. I know that sick husband of mine is in here" she replied. Angry woman turned and stormed through the door just as suddenly as she had appeared. Tyrone went back to pricing poppers keeping an eye on the cameras. Bitch was sitting in the parking lot for a while, and then she gave up and left.

Ryan came out of the back about 20 minutes later. He put a $50 on the counter and looked at Tyrone. Tyrone asked, "What can I get you?" "Nothing, thanks for the help and for fending off my bitch wife," Ryan replied. "What's the bill for," asked Tyrone. "A token of my thanks. That bitch has my cell phone tracked and I forgot to turn it off before I came in here," replied Ryan. "Oh, thank you," replied Tyrone. "You're welcome," replied Ryan. "I hope Vince goes well for you, he has a nice touch," he added. Tyrone laughed, and replied, "Thanks, good luck with that wife." "I think she's about to be downsized out of that job," Ryan replied. They both laughed as Ryan walked out the door.

9 781954 285033